PURE HELL WITH A GUN

Todd headed for the front door when a man almost as wide as he was tall suddenly blocked his way. He held a long-barreled Colt .44 in his right hand.

"Just hold it up there," the man said.

Todd had heard about whorehouses whose customers were robbed. His jaw tightened as he felt the tough's left hand dip into his pocket searching for Todd's roll of greenbacks. For an instant the man took his eyes off Todd's face—and that's all it took for Todd to grab the Colt with his left hand and shove the barrel away. At the same instant, Todd's Remington jumped into his right hand and the bore pressed against the man's chest.

"Wha . . . what're you going to do?" the tough said, standing rimrod-stiff. Only his lips moved.

"I don't know," Todd said, barely moving his own lips. "Blow your head off maybe."

CHEYENNE BROTHER

DOYLE TRENT

ZEBRA BOOKS
KENSINGTON PUBLISHING CORP.

ZEBRA BOOKS

are published by

Kensington Publishing Corp.
475 Park Avenue South
New York, NY 10016

First printing: December, 1988

Printed in the United States of America

CHAPTER ONE

He didn't see the danger until it was too late.

He'd been warned that the Cheyenne and Arapahoes in Colorado Territory hated white-eyes, and he thought he was being careful.

Todd Kildow was his name, but he had several aliases. He was on his way south from Wyoming where he'd helped deliver three thousand Texas longhorn cattle. He'd traded shots with the Arapahoes in western Kansas and the Comanches in Texas, and he thought he knew something about Indian tricks.

But the first thing he saw of this one was the bore of the rifle.

An icy fear jumped into his chest, and he knew he was too late as the red man pulled the trigger, but he dropped off his horse anyway. Slid off the right side away from the gun. Fell off.

The horse had never been mounted or dismounted from the right side, and it jumped sideways, jerking the pack horse with it.

He thought he was as good as dead. Out of habit—or instinct—he yanked his sixgun out of its holster the same instant he hit the ground, and thumbed the hammer back. He was determined to get in at least one shot before he died. But the horses were between him and the Indian and he couldn't shoot.

Then the horses jumped out of the way, and he had the red man's bare chest in his gunsight. His finger was tightening on the trigger.

He paused.

No shot had been fired. He hadn't been hit. And the Indian was having trouble. The rifle had misfired and the red man was trying desperately to lever another cartridge into the firing chamber. The magazine was blocked.

Shoot, his mind told him. Kill him. Shoot, damnit. He got to one knee and held the sixgun out at eye level.

The Indian was young. Around twenty. Hard to tell about an Indian. He wore britches of buckskin or antelope hide, leather moccasins with thin soles, and a white man's black wool vest, unbuttoned. No shirt. Course black hair hung down his back in a braid. He tried to work the lever on his long barreled rifle, and finally gave up. At first his eyes darted from side to side, looking for a place to take cover. He stood in a shallow, grassy draw where he had been hiding, but there was no protection there from a bullet.

Then his black eyes fixed on the white man, full of hatred. His mouth twisted in a grimace.

Todd Kildow took careful aim at the brown chest. No hurry. The man was unarmed and had nowhere to run. One bullet would do it. Shoot, his mind said.

The Indian's back stiffened, and he stood straight and proud, his arms at his sides, the rifle on the ground, waiting for death.

Shoot.

Naw.

The white man spoke. "I ought to put a bullet right between your murdering eyes. That's what you intended to do to me." It was the first time he'd spoken to another human in five days. He stood, backed up a couple of steps to where the red man couldn't jump him, and took a long careful look around.

The only living creatures in sight were his two horses. The country wasn't flat like western Kansas, but hilly. Low, rolling hills. Out of habit, his cattleman's eyes took in the grass. Plentiful and green. Tall wheat grass and short buffalo and gramma grass. A few trees stood away off in the distance. Probably cottonwoods. The ground was dotted with yucca and small bushes, a kind of bush he'd never seen before.

Were there more Indians around? This one had made himself invisible in the draw and there could be more of them. Indians had a way of making themselves invisible.

He studied every foot of the ground for a quarter mile around him. Nothing that breathed was in sight. Except this one. And his horses.

Slowly, he lowered the hammer on his Remington .44, the gun with the sawed-off five-and-a-half-inch barrel and the filed off front sight. It was a gun made for fast drawing and fast shooting.

"What the hell're you doing here all by yourself, anyway? Your tribe kick you out?"

The Indian only stared at him, eyes still full of hatred.

"Hell, you ain't got a horse or anything. Hell, you ain't even got a gun that'll shoot. What is it, a Henry? Yeah, that's what it is. Pretty good gun when it works, but doesn't always work. Bullets don't always fire, and if that tin magazine gets bent or gets a little dirt in it, it jams."

Still no sound from the Indian. They stared at each other. Todd was older, but only by a few years. They

7

were the same height and build, about five-eleven and slender. Perhaps the Indian was an inch shorter.

He was either Cheyenne or Arapahoe, one of the tribes that claimed eastern Colorado Territory. Hard to tell one from the other. He wore so few clothes that there was no clue there. Except maybe the moccasins. Yeah. Fancy colored porcupine quill flattened and woven into the toes in a rectangular design with two smaller rectangles. The white man had seen that design before. Cheyenne.

But while the red man was barechested, bareheaded and wore moccasins, the white man wore a wide-brim high-crown hat, a khaki shirt and riding boots. Boots and big Chihuahua spurs. And the white man's hair was light brown, almost blond. It stuck out from under the hat and bunched around his ears. His nose was straight and short and his mouth was wide, thin-lipped, over a square chin.

It was a face that, for most of his life, had always been ready to break into a grin, but now was habitually set in hard square lines.

"That sorry excuse for a lever gun saved my life. Thought you had a white man's scalp and a couple of horses, didn't you? Damn near did."

They continued staring at each other, and Todd noticed for the first time the scar on the Indian's right chest, nearly hidden by the vest. It was a long scar made by knife or bullet, the kind of wound that took a long time to heal. Finally the Indian moved his right hand, slowly deliberately, eyes still fixed on the white man's eyes. He drew a forefinger across his forehead, then with his hand in a fist he jerked it down and opened his fingers as if throwing something away. At the same time, his face twisted in anger.

"The hell you beller," Todd said. "Well hell, in

case you don't know it, I ain't too damn fond of you Indians either."

The Indian moved his right hand again, this time in a loose fist, back and forth across his chest several times.

"War, huh? If I was you, standing there with a jammed-up gun and nothing else, I wouldn't be talking about war."

Hands at sides now, the Indian stood proudly, waiting for whatever was to happen, and wanting the white man to know he was not afraid to die.

The white man studied him a moment, then drawled, "Well hell, maybe you're ready to meet your maker, but I believe I can find other things to do." Holding the Remington in his right hand, he let his left hand drop to his side, palm open, fingers straight. Then he jerked the hand up and shoved it forward. The Indian's expression changed from hatred to disbelief.

"Yeah, go on. Git. I can't shoot a man who can't shoot back." He repeated the motion with his left hand. "Go on, git."

Moving tentatively, the Indian turned half around, looked at the white man, took two steps, stopped and looked at the white man again.

"Git before I change my mind."

Another look of disbelief, then the Indian walked away, back straight.

"Hey, Todd yelled. "Hey, you forgot your gun." The Indian continued walking without looking back, heading south. Todd watched him for several moments, then said, "Aw well, it ain't worth a damn anyhow."

He caught his horses, mounted the bay, wrapped the pack horse's lead rope once around the saddle horn and passed the end under his right thigh to hold it. He sat his A-fork, rimfire saddle easily, like a man who has lived in a saddle, which indeed he had. The narrow iron stirrups fit into the shanks of his riding boots, and the rounded, hard leather shanks made them comfortable.

Hat brim pulled low to shield his eyes from the late afternoon sun, he watched the Indian walk away, then shook his head, wondering why the young savage was alone. Couldn't be lost. Indians didn't get lost.

He knew he should have killed him. Next time that young buck got a white man in his gunsights, his gun wouldn't jam. Should have dropped him and left his carcass right where it fell.

But he'd done all the killing he wanted to do.

First it was the war. His side had won, but winning cost a hell of a lot of good men. Dead or crippled for life. A bloody senseless war. That was three years ago. Then there were the two men he'd shot right where they'd sat at their campfire. That was only a year ago. He'd shot them without giving them a chance. Just aimed and fired his Spencer carbine, jacked another cartridge into the barrel and fired again.

Some gun, that Spencer. A .56 caliber. He'd fired once, then cocked the hammer back, swung down the finger lever, broken open the breech and slammed it shut again. That carried a cartridge from a magazine in the butt to the firing chamber. When the war ended and the troops were given an opportunity to buy their weapons, not many chose the Henry. It fired faster, but couldn't be depended on. The Spencer was the favorite.

Two shots and two men were hit. But it took too long to get off another shot. If he'd had one of the new Winchester repeating rifles, he'd have got all three.

And there was the man in Santa Fe, the Mexican with a knife. It was kill or be killed.

Now, he hoped he would never have to kill again. But he was a wanted man, and he was always searching, hanging around the toughs, gunslingers, thieves and killers wherever he could find them. Mixing with that kind was dangerous, and like it or not, a man had to defend himself. He'd traded the Spencer for the sawed-off Remington and practiced with it. Just in case.

Reining the bay south and west toward the purple mountains, he continued looking for a creek which, he'd been told, cut a wide canyon from the high country down to the plains.

The mountains looked closer than they really were, and as he rode toward them he realized he was farther east than he intended to be. He'd drifted almost straight south from Cheyenne, keeping on the plains, looking for the stream. It paralleled an old Ute Indian trail, he'd been told, and led to the gold fields in the Colorado high country. Up there men were getting rich digging and scratching in the rocks, or panning the creeks. Or from robbing and killing. And some weren't getting rich at all. Just breaking their backs swinging a pick and digging with a round-point shovel and finding nothing but granite.

It wasn't gold that Todd Kildow was looking for. He grinned inwardly as he realized he wouldn't know gold if he stumbled over it. It was a man. And when he thought of the man, his grin vanished and the hard lines came back to his face. He had practically no chance at all of finding him. Hell, he didn't know his name or even what he looked like. As he rode into the lowering sun, he tried for the thousandth time to recall what little he'd seen of the man.

11

There had been three of them. No doubt about their guilt. The black mare was tied to a tree, still carrying his dad's saddle. They were eating bread that his mother had baked fresh that day. Three of them, heavily armed, sitting near a fire back in the cottonwoods along the creek.

There was only one way to do it. If he'd called out, they would have started shooting, and he would have been lucky to get just one. No, he had surprise on his side, and he took advantage of it. Only the Spencer wouldn't fire fast enough, and one got away in the dark.

That one didn't show his face. Average size, average build, wearing a wide-brim hat like everyone else. No spurs on his boots. Just average. Nearly impossible to describe. Probably impossible to find. One of the two was dead, shot through the heart, and the other was dying. Todd had watched him die and tried to get information from him. The man couldn't—or wouldn't—talk. He'd left them there, untied the black mare and led her back to his own place. Then, long after dark, when everyone was in bed, he rode the ten miles to the town of Prairie, got the sheriff up and told him what had happened.

Sheriff R.M. Hocker. A strict law-and-order man.

Todd Kildow, now wanted for murder and jail break, rode into the Colorado foothills at sundown and began riding uphill among the granite boulders. He watered his horses in a creek, which he hoped was the one he was looking for, then went on until, just before dark, he came to a grassy park. There, he unsaddled, staked out his horses and made his camp. He was a little worried about the bay, a young horse that had been running wild only four months earlier. Todd kept an eye on him until the horse went to the end of the stake rope and turned back without fighting it. The horse had been staked out before, but he was green and easily spooked.

Supper was coffee boiled in a tin pot, thick slices of bacon fried over a wood fire and a can of peaches. One of those airtight cans that kept food from spoiling. He thought of the Indian down there on the plains with no gun, no knife, no blankets, no nothing. It made him grateful for his thin mattress and the bed tarp under the mattress and folded back over it. Three blankets. Even a pillow. But thinking of the Indian and how he hated white eyes prompted him to carry his bed back into the scrub oaks where he wouldn't be so easy to find.

Lying on his back with the Remington under the blankets beside him, he felt the old ache return. He didn't want to be a fugitive. God, how he wished the whole thing hadn't happened. For an hour he lay wide awake. The stars seemed to be bigger and brighter up here in the high country. Closer. A sliver of a quarter-moon showed itself on the eastern horizon. He wanted to go back, go on with his plans. For a couple of years after the war he'd been happy. He'd come home alive and healthy and he had a quarter-section of good farm and grassland. Too, there was plenty of public domain where he could graze cattle. Grass was stirrup-high now that the buffalo were thinned out. He'd had it all, and now he had nothing.

Groaning, he pulled his hat over his face and tried to sleep.

CHAPTER TWO

At daybreak he was up, seeing to his horses, leading them down to the creek to drink, building a fire and putting coffee on. By sunup he was mounted, riding uphill, trying to keep the creek in sight. The hills were so steep in places he had to stop every fifty feet and let his horses blow. When he joined the creek again, he saw it come down a canyon, and followed it upstream, hoping to find the Indian trail. There was no trail.

At mid-morning, he found himself in a canyon where the walls—layers upon layers of granite—rose almost straight up. Only a goat could travel through there. He had to turn his horses around and go back a half-mile to a spot where the canyon walls weren't so steep and so high. Even there it was a hard climb. Scrub oak grew thick in spots, and small twisted cedars had managed to sprout from the rocks. Up higher, the trees were tall and straight.

By noon, he had to admit he was following the wrong creek. There was nothing man-made, only a dim game trail where the going was hard. He could climb to the top of a ridge, and damned if there wasn't another rocky ridge across a valley just ahead. A man could wander around those hills for weeks without seeing a sign of a human.

15

At least the grass was good, and he off-saddled and let his horses graze and rest. Had to take care of the horses. A man on foot wouldn't last long. While the horses grazed, he started walking to the top of a rocky, timbered hill, hoping he could get high enough to see where he was. Puffing from the climb, he finally reached the top. All he saw was more ridges, valleys, hills and trees—pine and spruce and a few clumps of aspen. Below him, in a narrow valley, boulders as big as houses were piled on top of each other. The creek he had been following wound through the same valley. Beavers had built their dams in the creek, creating a string of small ponds. Like a string of pearls. Beautiful. Mother Nature made herself seen and felt more in the mountains. The high hills, the huge rocks, made a man seem terribly insignificant.

Away to the west was a range of mountains still covered with snow in places, and far to the south was a high peak, also white in spots. He stood there, trying to catch his breath in the high altitude and trying to decide which way to go. A small furry chipmunk ran from under a fallen tree and climbed to the top of a small boulder. It saw him and scurried back the way it had come. A raven flew past, and hearing its wings caused him to jerk his head down between his shoulders. Then he grinned at himself with relief. It sounded something like a cannonball going overhead.

That peak to the south, could it be Pikes Peak? It looked to be close to the foothills and it was high enough. He recalled the old slogan, "Pike's Peak or Bust," and another later one, "Pikes Peak Hoax." There'd been a lot of digging around the bottom of that peak, but not much gold was found. Instead, the new goldfields were farther north. That's what he'd been told.

Well, he either had to go on or go back. He had enough chuck to last a few more days. Grass for the horses was plentiful. And the mountain Indians, so he'd heard, weren't looking for white men's scalps.

He saddled up and rode on, back to the top of that hill and down into the green valley. Traveling was easy for a few miles, but then he had to climb again. Feeling sorry for the horses, he began looking for a good campsite two hours before sundown. In another green valley, along another stream—this one only a trickle in places—he staked his horses and gathered wood for a fire. Feeling restless, he walked again, stumbling over the rocks in his high-heeled riding boots, and thinking he ought to take off his spurs. In a spot where the willows grew thick along the creek, he pushed his way through, and climbed another hill.

Winded and leg-weary, he stopped at the top to sit on a small boulder. Behind him his horses grazed on the clump grass. He looked ahead, downhill, and suddenly jumped to his feet. Was that a road down there?

Eyes straining, he tried to make it out. If it was, it wasn't more than a couple of wagon tracks following still another creek through still another valley. It sure wasn't built by men with shovels and fresnos, but it looked passable, at least where it went through the valley. A road, all right, going east and west. Going where? To the goldfields? From Denver? He'd have to find out. Get his horses and go down there.

But not today. The sun was sitting on top of that range of mountains to the west. It would soon be dark. He'd wait until morning, then go and see where that road went.

Hell, who knows, it might lead to a town, the kind

17

of mining town that attracted a lot of strangers. Where men of all kinds came and went.

Where a fugitive from justice would feel safe.

The road, like the mountains, was farther away than it looked. The sun was halfway up to its peak when he topped a timbered hill and saw it below him. Just two tracks with grass growing between them, but well-traveled tracks. He could tell from their width and depth that many hooves and wagon wheels had created them. Across the road was about five acres of thick willows, and he guessed another stream ran through them. He dismounted and sat there awhile under a tall ponderosa, letting his horses rest. Soon he would get mounted again, go down to the road and follow it west. It had to lead somewhere.

He saw the willows move. Something was coming through. An animal, maybe? Deer or elk? Fascinated, he watched to see what it was, and when he saw it he couldn't believe it.

"Huh?" he snorted out loud. "What the humped-up hell?"

It was a man. Not just a man, but a man in his long-handled underwear. Just his long johns and boots. And a floppy hat. And a bandana around his neck. A man carrying a short shotgun. A sawed-off double-barreled shotgun.

Then another man came out, dressed the same way.

"What the hairy hell?" Were they camped on the other side of the bushes somewhere, and did they like to walk around in their underwear? Mighty strange ducks, those two.

They were looking down the road, looking east

toward Denver, and acting nervous, jumpy.

Todd Kildow pulled back slowly until he was lying on his stomach where he could see them, but where he himself would be hard to see. His horses were behind him, under the crest of the hill.

What the holy hell were those yahoos up to?

And then he knew.

He saw the stagecoach coming before they did. It was a Concord pulled by six trotting horses. The teamster had no doubt let the horses walk uphill and was trying to make time by keeping them at a trot in the valley. A shotgun messenger sat on the seat beside the teamster, with his hat pulled down and a double-barreled scatter-gun across his lap. The two yahoos heard it coming before they saw it, and they ducked back into the willows out of sight. But first, they pulled the bandanas up over their noses.

They were going to rob the stage.

It wasn't any of Todd Kildow's business. He couldn't just lope down there and scare them away. He could fire a shot in the air and warn the driver and guard. But if he did, the two ducks in their long johns would be very unhappy with him, and he didn't want to have to outrun two angry men with sawed-off shotguns. The stage line could damn well take care of itself. He watched.

Sure enough. When the stage was within twenty feet, the two jumped out with their guns leveled and yelling, "Hold up. Whoa right there."

The guard started to swing his long-barreled gun in their direction, and stopped when he found himself looking into the bore of a gun that couldn't miss. One blast from that gun would take his head off.

The teamster whoaed his team and pushed the brake lever forward with his right foot.

19

"Throw up your hands."

They were on each side of the lead team now. The horses were snorting and stamping, nervous. A gunshot would make them hard to handle.

"Throw down that shotgun."

The guard's gun hit the ground, and his hands were up.

"Throw down the strong box."

"Ain't no strong box. We ain't carryin' nothin' but passengers."

"You're a liar." A short scatter-gun was still aimed at the guard. "You. Git down. Climb down from there." The guard did as he was told. He had no choice. His death would accomplish nothing.

On the ground, he was patted down and a six-shooter was taken from his right boot. "On your belly, face down." He lay down.

"You." One of the two robbers had opened the coach door and was pointing his gun inside. "Git out of there. Git your asses out of there before I shoot 'em off."

He stepped back to allow three men and a woman to climb out. "Line up there."

The other thug was now in position to watch everyone, and he kept his gun level and ready to fire. The first one got into the coach and began tearing up the floorboards. "It's here. I know goddamned well it is. They always hide it." Then he let out a happy yell. "Here it is. God damn." He backed out, dragging a small metal case with him.

"Open it. Let's see what we got."

"Keep your eyes on them sons-of-bitches." The slit in the back of his long johns spread as he bent over the suitcase, exposing his bare behind. He didn't even notice as he concentrated on prying open the suitcase with a long knife. When he straightened, he

20

held up a handful of greenbacks.

"Goddamn." He slammed the lid shut and snapped the lock. "Let's go."

"Not yet. This gent's got a full wallet, I'm bettin'." The second hoodlum was looking at a well-groomed man in a homburg hat, finger-length dark coat, wool pants with a crease down the front and a gold watch chain draped across a flowery vest. The gentleman was clean-shaven with a thin moustache over a narrow mouth. "Let's have it."

Without hesitation, the man took a thick cowhide wallet from a pocket inside his coat and handed it over. His hands were shaking, and he said nothing.

"Well, well, what else we got here. Ever'body hand it over. You too, lady."

He snatched wallets and he snatched the woman's handbag, and for the first time he took a good look at the woman. "Say, you're purty."

From his spot on the hill, Todd Kildow agreed. She had chestnut hair under a little pillbox lacy hat, wide eyes, a straight nose and a mouth with just enough curve and color to make her one of the prettiest young women he had ever seen. She stared at the hoodlum, looking him right in the eye.

The hoodlum glanced around. The guard was still down on his belly and the teamster had his hands full of leather lines. Everyone was at his mercy. "Yes sir, you're one damn purty woman. Bet you got a good figger under that long dress." He stepped closer and shifted the gun to his right hand. "Let's just have us a feel."

She backed up against the coach. Her eyes were no longer bold. Now they were terrified. "Please," she said, and then she said it again, louder, "Please."

That was when Todd Kildow drew the Remington.

CHAPTER THREE

He couldn't hit a target at that range with the short-barreled six gun, and if he missed the man in long johns he'd hit one of the passengers, maybe the woman. Todd aimed over their heads, over the top of the coach, and squeezed the trigger. The short Remington boomed like a cannon. The sound crashed among the hills.

For a second everyone froze. Then one of the hoodlums spun around and fired a blast from the shotgun. The lead pellets fell short and did no harm. But the gunfire spooked the team, and the driver was hauling back on the lines. "Whoa. Whoa, now."

Todd fired again, not trying to hit anyone. The recoil from the Remington smacked the palm of his hand, and he liked the feel of it. That did it. One of the yahoos in long johns snatched up the metal case and headed on a run around the coach. The second one followed. They disappeared into the willows.

"Whoa. Whoa, you damn fools." The teamster had his hands full and couldn't go after them.

But the guard could. He jumped up, grabbed his shotgun off the ground and went on a lope around the coach after the robbers. He paused, fired one barrel, and resumed running into the willows. The passengers hurried around the coach to watch. All but one.

"Whoa, fools. Whoa damnit."

She looked up the hill at Todd. He rose to one knee. Their eyes locked. Wide gray eyes and pale blue ones. For a long moment, they stared at each other. Her face showed no expression. Then he stood and went back under the crest of the hill toward his horses.

As he mounted, he heard another blast from a shotgun, and he heard the teamster pleading, "Whoa, now. Whoa."

One thing he didn't want was to be a hero. Heroes drew attention. That was the last thing he needed. Why did he let that young woman get a good look at him? Why? Well, because she was the prettiest woman he'd ever seen, and he couldn't help staring at her. But it was a dumb thing to do.

He turned his horses away from the road and traveled a half-mile south of it. There, he dismounted in a clump of aspens and watched his back trail. No one came after him. An hour later, he mounted again and rode back the way he'd come. At the top of the hill he paused and saw that the coach was gone. He went on, his horses sliding at times on the steep hill, and stopped on the road. Lots of footprints, but nothing else. He wondered if anybody had been shot, and he wondered if the young woman had gotten her pocketbook back. No way of knowing.

Well, at least the traveling was easier here, and he urged his horses on. The pack horse was carrying a light load and was easy to lead.

At noon, he stopped, let his horses rest and ate a cold meal. A string of eight freight wagons went past, going east. He had an urge to ask the teamsters where they came from and what was ahead, but instead he merely waved and kept his distance. He'd find out soon enough.

The next man-made objects he saw were a long log cabin, two corrals holding a dozen horses and two toilets behind the cabin. It had to be a relay station for the stage line. The story of the robbery had been told there, and the story included the unseen man on the hill who had scared the robbers away. Unseen, except by the woman. Did she describe him? Probably.

Boy, he could use a good meal, and meals were probably sold there. But it wouldn't do to ride over and let everyone get a good look at him. They'd recognize him from the woman's description and they'd be full of questions.

Going around and staying out of sight meant climbing more hills and scrambling over more rocks, and it took two hours to get back to the road. Once there, he got his horses into a trot and kept it up until a couple of hours before dark. Then it was another lonely camp, a tin of dried beef, a handful of dried apricots and coffee. Well, if a man had to camp out, the mountains was a good place to do it. Grass and water were everywhere. Snowmelt from that range of mountains to the west created a hundred narrow streams. A good place to camp in the summer, but in the winter those mountains were man-killers, he'd been told.

Again, he unrolled his bed back in the trees away from the campfire. He didn't want anybody sneaking up on him. Not that anybody was likely to up here. But no use taking chances. As usual, he had trouble dropping off to sleep.

The jail in Prairie, Kansas. He'd never forget that jail. Four cells, three of them occupied. Sheriff Hocker didn't stand for any hooligans or vigilantes in Prairie County and he never passed up a chance to lock somebody up. He was elected because he promised to enforce the law and put nobody above the law. Todd's neighbors assured him he had nothing to worry about. He was entitled to a trial before a jury of his peers, and nobody in Prairie County was going to convict him for what he did. But that got to be a little hard to swallow when the lawyer came around.

You can't second-guess a jury, the lawyer had said. A smart prosecuting attorney can make a jury believe anything. Don't bet your life on what a jury will do. You need a good trial lawyer to represent you. You can pay for legal counsel, can't you?

And the boredom. Nothing to do but pace back and forth in his small cell like a caged animal, using a bucket for a toilet. Wait for a circuit judge to get there. It was enough to drive a man plumb out of his mind. One of the other prisoners did go crazy and started banging his head against the steel bars. He had to be chained to his bunk. But the other one, he was a cool son-of-a-gun. Never made a sound. Just waited. He was the youngest of the three Greener brothers from the Indian Nation to the south. The Greeners were bank- and stage-robbers. He just waited with a small smile on his face.

The night wind whispered through the tall pines over his head, and Todd Kildow groaned and turned over on his side. What the bare-assed hell could a man do?

He had breakfast over and was getting ready to load the skillet, coffeepot and groceries back into a pannier when he next saw the Indian.

"Huh." Todd grunted, startled. The Remington

jumped into his hand. The Indian didn't flinch. Didn't even blink. He was squatting on his heels fifty feet away near a four-foot-high boulder. "What . . . ?"

Todd recognized him. The leather britches, the black wool vest, the scar along his right side. Only now, his expression was blank. No hatred, no curiosity, no nothing. Round black eyes stared at him. No gun, no knife.

"Where in hell did you come from?"

No answer.

"How long you been sitting there?"

No movement.

"Well, what do you want?"

The eyes moved then, taking in the slab of bacon that Todd was about to wrap in a piece of canvas. The expression didn't change.

"Hungry? Hell, I thought you Indians could eat anything. Even rattlesnakes. And I thought you could spit fire to cook 'em with. Or eat 'em raw."

The black eyes were fixed on the bacon.

"You really hungry? Well, I can't let anything starve." He holstered his six-gun and used a long butcher knife to cut a three-inch slice off the slab of bacon. "Need fire to cook it with? All right." He rebuilt the fire.

The Indian didn't move, only stared.

"What else do you need? Can't give you a gun. You'd probably shoot me with it. Need a knife? Well, I just happen to have an extra one."

Still no sound or movement from the Indian as Todd rummaged through one of the two panniers and located the skinning knife. It was a fancy one with a handle made of antelope horn, whetted as sharp as a razor and sheathed in a homemade leather holster with a fringe down the side. Colored porcupine quills had been woven into the leather in a rectangular pattern. He tossed it to the Indian. That got a reaction.

The redman grabbed it from where it fell on the ground, turned it over, looked at Todd and said something in Indian language.

"What? Oh yeah, I know it's an Indian knife. I've been carrying it for a year now and never had any use for it."

More Indian language.

"What are you so excited about? You might as well be talking Greek."

The Indian doubled his right hand, held it chin high and brought it down slowly as if holding something in his fist.

"What? Oh, I get it. Maybe I do. You're saying it's your knife. Is that it? Naw, couldn't be."

When the young red man stood, the Remington appeared again in Todd's right hand. "Whoa. Stay right there. Don't come any closer with that frog-sticker."

Neither moved for a moment; then the Indian squatted again. Todd holstered his gun and went on loading his groceries in the panniers and hanging them on the crossbucks of the pack saddle. His folded bed went on top of the load, and, keeping an eye on the savage, Todd threw a box-hitch to hold the load on the pack horse. He mounted his saddle horse and was ready to leave.

"Don't sneak up on me like that anymore. I've got a nervous trigger finger." Reining his horses toward the road, he said. "Adios," and rode away.

He had to go around another stage-line relay station, up and down two rocky hills, through a mile of thick timber and across a grassy, boggy meadow. He dismounted on the edge of the meadow and let the horses eat the tall swamp grass while he consumed a tin of dried beef. He couldn't get the Indian out of his mind.

Was he following Todd? Naw. No reason in the world he'd be doing that. But where was he going, and what was he doing? Strange. More damned strange things happening.

When he got horseback again and back on the road, he saw a wagon coming from the east, pulled by two horses. It carried a man and woman and some furniture, including an iron bedstead and an iron four-hole cookstove. This time Todd stayed on the road.

"Morning," he said when the man "whoaed" his team. "Or is it afternoon?"

"Howdy. Headin' for White River?"

"Yeah, reckon I am. Any idea how far it is?"

The woman, a little plump in a plain cotton dress with a black wool bandana over her head, let the man do the talking.

"Said back there she's about twelve mile. Gonna do some prospectin'?"

"I don't know. I wouldn't know gold or silver if it bit me."

The man's eyes in a thin, wrinkled face went over Todd's riding boots and spurs and settled for a moment on the six-gun carried low. His eyes narrowed, and his hands on the lines tightened. "You, uh, look like a cattleman. Is cattle your business?"

"Wish it was, but I'm just a hired hand."

"Just driftin', huh?"

The woman had noticed the Remington too, and was nervously pulling at her shawl.

Todd saw the effect he was having on the couple. He tried to say something to put them at ease. "Yeah, kind of a foolish thing to do." He shrugged, and picked up on his reins. "Here's wishing you-all a lot of luck." He reined his horse off the road.

"Good luck to you too, mister." The man clucked to the team, and the wagon began rolling again.

Todd kept his horses still until it was out of sight around a line of willows.

He didn't want to overtake the wagon, and he estimated he could travel the twelve miles riding at a walk and get to White River before sundown. The road led over a long hill, downhill, across a narrow creek, down a valley and over another long hill. Todd could see the wagon ahead of him as the team labored to pull it up the hill. Then he saw a stagecoach coming from the west, pulled by a six-up. Again, he stayed on the road. He couldn't keep out of sight forever. The stage went past on a high trot with singletrees rattling and horses blowing. Todd, the teamster and the shotgun messenger merely waved at each other.

Riding on, Todd went through two miles of thick timber, tall pine and spruce, and enjoyed the sweet smell of it. Out of the timber, he rode between boulders as big as a castle, then climbed another long hill. At the top he stopped to let his horses blow, and looked down on a town a mile away.

No one-horse town, this. It covered a section of land, and it sat on the south edge of a gently sloping, heavily timbered hill that climbed for miles and miles.

There were a half-dozen two-story buildings on either side of a main street, and at least ten smaller buildings with false fronts and a boardwalk in front of them. More houses than a man could count, and from where he sat, they looked to be made of good lumber. Smokestacks belched black smoke on the south side, and mine dumps surrounded the town on three sides. Todd counted eight mine headframes sticking up treetop high, and he guessed there were more that he couldn't see. A river, wide but shallow, ran between the town and the timbered hill.

He took it all in, then touched spurs to his horse's sides. "Let's get down there and see what there is to see," he said to the horses. "Down there is good hay and maybe some grain, and a woman-cooked supper, and a soft bed and, hell, no telling what else."

The horses moved on, glad to be going downhill instead of up. He continued talking to them.

"No sir, no telling what I might find. Maybe even . . . aw, who the jammed-up hell knows?"

CHAPTER FOUR

While he was making his way to town—his eyes trying to take in everything—another stagecoach came snorting and clattering from behind him. The six-horse team was urged into a gallop going downhill and then down onto the main street. The teamster wanted to arrive at a run, cracking his long whip and yelling at the horses. From where he was, still on the outskirts, Todd could see everyone getting out of the way of the coach, and he could see the coach come to a stop in front of a three-story wood-frame building. He saw people gather around, helping to unload luggage and mail sacks from the coach.

A large sign on the outskirts read: WHITE RIVER, COLORADO POPULATION 3,000 AND GROWING.

Growing was right. Wooden frameworks for new buildings lined the main street, and new houses were going up everywhere. The whine of a sawmill came from the south side, and a steam whistle sounded from over on the west. Long wagons pulled by four-ups hauled timbers to the sawmill, and smaller freight wagons and buckboards passed each other on the streets. Horseback riders rode at a walk or a trot, and pedestrians, men in all kinds of clothes from bib overalls and slouchy hats to creased pants and spats, occupied the plank sidewalk. The men stepped aside politely to make room for a few women in long dresses.

It was an hour or so until dark, and Todd rode the length of the main street and back again to the east side. No one paid any attention to him. Strangers were no oddity. His horses were a little nervous at all the people and activity; their heads were up and their ears were twitching, but they were not hard to handle.

The main street offered just about every kind of product and service a man could want. He rode past two cafés, a laundry, two hotels, three saloons, a boarding house, two mercantiles, a harness and saddle shop, a barbershop and a butcher shop with a hand-painted sign advertising fresh beef.

A livery barn a block off the main street was easy to spot, and Todd reined over there. "Evening," he said to a man in baggy wool pants pushing a wheelbarrow of manure out of the barn.

Without much more than a glance, the man answered, "Evenin'."

"Are you the proprietor?"

Grunting, the answer came, "Yep." He dumped the wheelbarrow load on a pile of manure beside the barn.

"Got feed for a couple more horses?"

"Yep." He dropped the wheelbarrow and mopped his face with a red polka-dot bandana. He had a handlebar moustache and two days' growth of beard. "You'll have to keep 'em outside, howsomever. Ain't no more room in the barn."

Todd grinned. "These old ponies have never seen the inside of a barn anyhow. This pack horse is a cannibal, though. He'll fight strange horses."

"Haveta keep 'em in that little pen over there,

then." He took off his floppy hat and pointed with it to a half-dozen pole corrals behind the barn. "I don't wanta get somebody else's horse kicked. There's water piped into that tank, and you can throw 'em some good mountain grass from that stack over there."

"Just what I need. How much?"

"Two bits a day, and if you wanta give 'em a bait of oats it's another dime. You can put your saddles and outfit in the barn. I always lock the barn at night."

"Good enough."

"You buyin' cattle or somethin'?"

"No. I'm just curious about what's going on around here. I hear men are getting rich digging holes in the ground."

"Some are. Most ain't."

Todd saw a chance to ask the question he'd asked a hundred times in the past year. "Lots of strangers come through here, I reckon."

"Folks come and go."

"Seen anybody from Kansas?"

"They come from all over. You from Kansas?"

"No," Todd answered quickly. "I'm from Texas. Just helped trail three thousand cattle to Wyoming, and decided to stop by here on my way back. See what the excitement's all about."

"Thought you looked like a Texican." the faded eyes squinted at Todd. "How come you're lookin' for somebody from Kansas?"

"Oh, uh . . ." Todd had to think fast. "I know a man that came from Kansas, and I thought he might be here. He said once he was going to Colorado and dig for gold."

"What's he look like?"

"Well, he's, uh, about my size and he's got an ordinary face. He'd be hard to describe."

35

The stableman shook his head. "Wal, I can't help you with no more to go on than that."

Todd grinned a wry grin. "He probably isn't even here. I'll just put my horses in that pen and throw 'em some hay. You want to get paid now or later?"

"Better pay me now before you lose your cash in the Gold Palace. They got a way of separatin' men from their money in there."

Fishing a dollar out of his pocket, Todd said, "This'll pay for a few days." He grinned again. "I don't know what the Gold Palace is like, but I've been in gambling dives before."

"You ain't seen this one."

"Yeah, well, I found out long ago that I'm not the smartest card player there is."

His boot heels thumped on the plank sidewalk, and his Mexican spurs made crunching, clicking sounds, as he walked to a hotel sign that hung over the walk. He was carrying a canvas warbag containing a change of clothes, a shaving mug, razor, strop and small mirror. He passed at least a dozen pedestrians, and nobody gave him a second glance. That was good and bad. White River was a good place for a fugitive to get lost, but it was a bad place to look for someone he couldn't name.

The first hotel he came to was new and luxurious. Todd stopped in the door to look around. The lobby was as big as a barn with a thick carpet, plush leather armchairs, and dark red velvet wallpaper. A big desk across the room had to have been hand-carved of mahogany. Adjacent to that was a spiral staircase to the second floor. Behind the desk was a little man in a dark coat with a cravat. His face was businesslike. Todd decided not to go in.

Instead he walked another block and went into a two-story building with a sign out front that read:

PONDEROSA HOTEL. This one had a small lobby with a plain wooden floor, two hard chairs, and a pine desk. The stairs were straight with no bannister. The man behind the desk wore a striped shirt and a mean expression on his face. This was something Todd was used to.

A wise, squinty pair of eyes peered over half-glasses and went over Todd from the warbag on his shoulder, to the Remington, to the riding boots and spurs. "We don't allow no drinking in the rooms and we don't allow no rowdies, and we have to be paid in advance."

"Have you got a bathtub?"

"Yeah, but you carry your own hot water from that tank out back. Rooms are four bits a night. If you stay long enough we change the linens once a week."

Grinning, Todd said, "I take it you don't have to advertise much."

"We don't allow no smart alecks, either. If you don't want to abide by our rules, there's a cot house two blocks south."

Todd's grin turned to a chuckle. "How can I turn down a sales pitch like that? Do I sign a register, or something?"

The little man opened a wide book and pointed to a page. "You sign here, and we don't allow no bogus names, either."

"Wouldn't think of it." Todd had already decided on a name and he put down the warbag and signed the register as Douglas Brock, Amarillo, Texas.

Turning the book so he could read it, the little man squinted at the signature, then turned the book back, "You have to state your business too."

Todd shook his head, but grinned. "I'm not applying for citizenship or anything. All I want is a room."

"We don't allow no smart alecks. State your business or go elsewhere."

"Yeah, yeah." He wrote "Prospector" opposite the name, half-expecting the little man to snort and order him out.

"You pay now."

"All right, all right, here's a couple of dollars. That's good for four days, huh?"

"Only if you behave yourself and don't bother our other roomers."

"Wouldn't think of it."

He was handed a key as long as his forefinger and was told that the bathtub was in a room behind the desk, and the hot water tank and toilet were out back.

"We don't allow no chamber pots in the rooms."

"I could have guessed that."

The room, on the second floor, was surprisingly clean and neat, with an iron bedstead, a soft mattress, clean white sheets and a table that held a pitcher of water and a wash basin. There were even hooks on the wall where he could hang his clothes. Todd parted the white lace curtains to look out of the room's only window at the street below. After sleeping out for months, it was going to take a while to get used to sleeping in a room near a noisy street.

But, he thought as he took another look at the soft bed, it won't take very long.

Someone had a fire going under the water tank behind the hotel, and Todd carried six bucketsful to the five-foot-long tin bathtub inside. Then he had to pump six bucketsful from a hand pump to refill the hot water tank. He soaked in the tub a long time and washed himself thoroughly with a bar of smelly yellow soap. In his room, he stropped his razor and used the wash basin and his own mirror to shave.

Looking at himself in the mirror, he allowed he'd

have to get a haircut now. With a fresh shave and long hair he looked like a woman. Well, an old woman. By then it was two hours after dark. The barbershop was no doubt closed for the day. The clothes he took from his warbag were wrinkled, but clean. Cotton duck pants and a muslin shirt. The pants had a double layer of material on the seat and inside the thighs to make them wear longer on horseback. Clean shorts and socks make him feel like a new man.

He grinned at his growling stomach. "Let's you and me go find us a woman-cooked meal."

Out of curiosity, he stopped in front of the fancy hotel and studied the handwritten menu pasted inside a glass window. Seems the hotel had its own restaurant where fine cuisine was served. Cocktails too.

What the red-assed hell, Todd wondered, is a cuisine? And what's a cocktail? Sounded like a fancy cake with a long feather stuck in it. No place for a working man.

He found a cafe more to his liking two doors down. The Denver Steak House. Inside, he sat at a long counter, studied the menu tacked to a wall behind the counter and ordered a Kansas City steak with mashed potatoes and brown gravy. The waitress was middle-aged with a long dress, a white apron and a tired look on her face.

Only three stools were vacant, and Todd had chosen the middle one where he would have some elbow room. But not for long. He no more than ordered when a short, thick man with a wild beard, overalls and jackboots plopped down beside him. Both men were silent until after the bearded one ordered a steak; then Todd tried the same old questions.

"Pardon me, mister, are you acquainted here?"

"I know a few folks. Not many. You lookin' fer somethin'?"

"Yeah, I met a man in Texas who said he was coming here. He's from Kansas."

"What's his John-Henry?"

Todd pretended to ponder the question. "Danged if I know. He told me once, but I disremember. He's about my size and he looks a lot like me."

Shaking his head, the bearded one said, "Lots of men your size. Ever'body around here is from somewhere else. They come from ever'where."

"Well, he might not be here. Just thought you might have met sombody my size from Kansas."

Hot coffee was served then in thick china mugs, and both men concentrated on that. The bearded one slurped his. Todd sipped quietly and tried to listen to the conversations of other men at the counter.

"Old George was diggin' a basement and hit a vein. Sold 'er for ten grand. Now he's goin' back to Illinois to fetch his woman and kids."

"Who bought 'er?"

"That dandy at the Gold Palace, that Hays feller."

"Oh, him. Ever'thing he touches spouts money."

"He'll make a million out of 'er, you bet."

"Lost a wad in that stage robbery, but he'll never miss it."

"Wish she'd hurry up with that steak. My stomach thinks my throat's plugged up."

Conversation died when the middle-aged woman began delivering platters of food. Todd enjoyed his meal immensely, and cleaned his platter. He ordered a hunk of peach pie which was supposed to have been made with fresh peaches. Tasted like canned fruit, but the crust made it mighty good anyway. Stomachs full, conversation resumed.

"Seen that purty woman that was robbed on the stage? She's from a rich family in Texas, I hear."

"She got her pocketbook back, didn't she? Way I heard it somebody took a shot at the robbers and chased 'em away so fast they left her satchel or whatever it was behind."

"That's what I heard too. But they got away with a box full of greenbacks that was headed for the bank. Old Kessler blasted at 'em with his scatter-gun and he thinks he winged one, but he ain't certain."

"I heard she come to White River to hunt for her kid sister."

"You don't say? Wal, she oughten to be hard to find. Ain't too many women around here."

Todd paid for his meal and went back out onto the sidewalk. Seemed he wasn't the only one in town looking for somebody. But the pretty woman knew her sister's name and what she looked like.

I hope, Todd mused as he walked down the board-walk, boots thumping and spurs chinging, she has better luck than I've had.

41

CHAPTER FIVE

He couldn't have missed the Gold Palace if he'd tried. Four bright lanterns hung outside the door; the door itself was big enough to drive a stagecoach through and was wide open. The lanterns outside and the lamplight from inside illuminated the sidewalk and street in front of the place. Horses were tied to a hitchrail, and two buggy teams were standing next to hitching posts. A piano tinkled inside, but was barely heard above the haw-haws and hum of voices. A woman's shrill laughter rose above the other sounds.

The place drew men like a magnet. They came and went, talking, laughing, cursing.

Todd stepped aside to let two men pass, then stepped inside. He had to pause a long moment to let his eyes take it all in. Some dive.

First it was the bar itself. Had to have been a good forty feet long, hand carved oak with a brass footrail and a half-dozen spittoons. The mirror behind the bar was as long as the bar. It had been put together in sections, but Todd had to look closely to see where the sections joined. There were the paintings above the mirror. Naked ladies. One was on her stomach with the biggest, roundest pair of haunches Todd could imagine. Another was standing with her hands

43

crossed in front of her crotch, but showing bare breasts. And still another was bending over, buttoning a pair of high-top shoes. The shoes were the only clothes she had on.

Fascinating to a man who hadn't even been close to an attractive woman for months.

There were gaming tables. All handcarved oak with felt covers on top, surrounded by solidly built wooden chairs. Four were occupied by men playing cards. There was a faro table and a roulette wheel. Men around them. And the women. The women wore dresses that were low at the top and short at the bottom, and they wore fishnet stockings and fancy garters. The war paint they had on was enough to decorate a whole tribe of Cheyenne.

Fresh sawdust covered the rest of the floor, and knotty pine panels covered the walls. Across from the bar was a carpeted staircase that led to the second floor. A big man with shoulders two axe-handles wide stood at the bottom. He caried a short club on the left side of his belt and a six-gun on the right side. His face looked as if it had been kicked in when he was a growing boy and had never straightened out.

Todd made his way to the bar, sidestepping to avoid collisions, and tried to get a bartender's attention. Two bartenders in striped shirts with garters on their sleeves were working as fast as they could, drawing beer from a keg and pouring whiskey.

"Yessir," one of them said, stopping in front of Todd.

"Uh, a beer," Todd said. In ten seconds he had it, in a thick glass with a handle on it.

"Ten cents."

"Huh?" Oh well, he thought, it's worth it just to get a look at his place. He took a short, tentative

44

swallow, then another long one. The beer was cold and good. He wondered how they kept it so cold.

"Hello, cowboy." She was pretty in an over-painted sort of way, and she smelled delicious. "You look like you've been out in the hills a long time. Would you buy a lady a drink?"

"Huh? Oh, sure." He couldn't keep his eyes away from that deep V between her breasts.

Somehow, the bartender was right there with a bottle in his hand. He poured a shot glass full, and she picked it up and threw it down her throat in one quick movement.

"Four bits."

Todd started to say "Huh?" again, but swallowed hard instead.

"Where you from, cowboy?"

She was standing so close their elbows touched. It sent a tingle through Todd's arm. "I, uh, I'm from, uh, Texas."

"I should have guessed." When she smiled she wasn't so pretty. Her teeth crossed themselves and were blue in spots. "Looking for a game?"

"No, uh, I just got in town."

"Are you selling cattle?"

"No, I'm looking for a gent I met in Texas. He's from Kansas and he's about my size."

"He owe you some money?"

"No, he said he was going up to Colorado to prospect for gold, and I wondered if he was around here."

"Could be. I could use another drink."

"Sorry. I, uh, I've got to go." He turned toward the door.

"Come back anytime, cowboy."

"Shoo." He sighed as he stepped out onto the sidewalk. A man could spend his money right fast in

45

there. His shoulder collided with another man who staggered out. "Whup."

"'S'matter with you? Can't you see where you're goin'?"

"I can, but I'm not so sure about you."

"You wanna fight?" He staggered back three steps, forward two steps and sideways another step. His fists came up in a fighting position, but then he staggered sideways again.

Grinning, Todd said, "No. I believe I'll pass up that invitation."

"That hogleg you're packin' don't scare me none." His eyes grew shrewd as they took in the Remington, the boots and spurs. "I'll bet you're from Texas. You Texas cowprods think you're tough."

"No," Todd said, wanting to get away from the drunk. "We're no tougher than we have to be."

"Well, I'm from Kansas, and us Kansas fellers are just as tough as any damn body."

"You what? When did you leave Kansas?"

"Last spring. So what?"

"Where in Kansas did you come from?"

"Kansas damn City, that's where. So what?"

"Who'd you come with?"

"Me and my whole famdamnly. Two kids and a woman."

"Aw hell." Todd's interest faded. "Know anybody else from Kansas?"

"Shore. Us Kansans're gonna whip the shit out of you Texans and take over Colorada Territory. Put 'em up."

"Naw. I've got a hunch, when you get home, you're gonna get all the fighting you want."

The drunk's expression changed suddenly from belligerence to fright. "Gawddamn. I was s'posed to of been home two hours ago. My old woman's gonna kill me. Jaysus Christ." He staggered away, muttering, "She's gonna skin me alive and . . . Jaysus B. Christ."

"Shooo." Todd sighed. He turned toward the Ponderosa Hotel. So far he'd learned exactly nothing. He was wasting his time. His money wouldn't last forever either. Well, he'd hang around a few days and then . . . then what?

Get a job, work a couple of months, move on, ask questions, move on.

"Damn," he muttered. "This thing has got to come to an end one of these days."

The soft bed wasn't as comfortable as he thought it would be. It was a feather bed. Too soft. He felt like he was going to suffocate. After half an hour he wished he'd brought his bedroll up to the room. He could sleep better in it on the floor.

Two quick gunshots down on the street brought him out of bed with a jump and a snort. He took three long steps to the window and looked down. A small crowd of men had gathered. One was holstering a six-gun. Another was flat on his back with two men kneeling over him. The survivor of the fight was the big pug-faced gent Todd had seen standing at the bottom of the stairs in the Gold Palace. He walked away as if nothing had happened. Three men followed him.

Standing in the dark hotel room, Todd watched as a tall, thin gent in a black coat hurried up. Todd couldn't hear what was said. He saw the tall man kneel beside the man on his back, put an ear to his chest, then stand and shake his head. When he half turned and looked up the street, Todd saw the silver law officer's star on his coat, over his heart.

It didn't take long for the excitement to fade down there. Two men carried the dead man away, and the

47

lawman left, going back the way he'd come. Soon the crowd left too.

It was as bad as Santa Fe. Men killed each other and walked away. Killings happened almost every day. That's why Todd had traded for the Remington and practiced with it. He'd driven a four-mule team pulling a heavy freight wagon to Santa Fe from Amarillo. It was a job, and it kept him moving. The route he'd taken with fourteen other teams and wagons was a well-traveled trade route, but the Comanches attacked anyway. They'd hit a wagon train, fire their rifles and keep up the attack until the teamsters managed to get on the other side of their wagons and shoot back. Then the Indians booted their ponies into a high lope out of rifle range.

At times, the teamsters could see bunches of Indians off in the distance, watching them. No telling when they'd attack. "Keep them long guns ready, boys," the wagon boss had said every hour or so, riding his sorrel horse back and forth from one end of the wagon train to the other. Two teamsters, both from Misssouri, were killed in an Indian fight four days from Santa Fe. Their bodies were buried on the prairie.

Todd had stayed in Santa Fe two weeks, asking the same questions. He left in the middle of the night on a horse he'd bought only the day before. A Mexican was threatening to cut him up in little pieces and feed him to the coyotes, and the Remington had fired almost by itself. It was a clear case of self-defense, but who knows what the law will do? Besides, Todd didn't want any lawman asking questions.

Back to Amarillo, keeping his eyes open for Comanches, lucky enough to stay out of their sight. In Amarillo he hired out on a big cow outfit being put together by two brothers from Scotland. The cowboys eyed the Remington and warned him that if he ever drew the gun, he'd be fired immediately, and if he shot anybody, he'd be hung from the nearest tree. Todd kept the gun in his warbag until he left four months later; then he fired a few practice shots with it and headed south to Fort Worth.

At Fort Worth he asked the usual questions and got nowhere. When he heard about the big cattle gather and the drive to Wyoming, he hired on.

The rest of the night was quiet, and Todd finally dozed off. Being indoors, he didn't awaken until an hour after daylight, and it took a few seconds to remember where he was. He washed his face, combed his hair, decided he'd get a haircut, and stomped downstairs and over to the livery pens to feed his horses. Then back to the Denver Steak House.

Conversation was light as men hurried through their meal, eager to get to the goldfields and strike it rich. The hired miners had already had breakfast and were down in the shafts and stopes, drilling and mucking. Todd's fried eggs were delicious, and out of curiosity he asked the middle-aged waitress how they kept them fresh.

"You ain't spent a winter in Colorada, have you?" she asked, picking up dirty dishes.

"No. Just got here."

"Well, I'll tell you, there's one thing we got plenty of and that's ice. And with the sawmills goin' full blast, we got plenty of sawdust to keep it frozen."

"Oh. Sure is good."

"Where're you from?"

Todd decided to change his story, at least this once. "Kansas. I reckon there's lots of folks from Kansas around here."

49

"There's folk from everywhere." She had a double armload of dirty dishes by then and she carried them to the kitchen.

Outside, on the plank walk, he spotted the barber's striped pole, and made his way over there, sidestepping to keep from colliding with other pedestrians. Just like Santa Fe. One damn busy town. Only here, the freight wagons weren't hauling trade goods, but were loaded with crushed ore or long timbers. In the barbershop, he read the *Police Gazette* while he waited his turn in the barber chair. The man who occupied it now was freshly shaved and had a steaming white towel wrapped around his face with only his nose sticking out. His black boots were polished to a shine, and his wool pants had a sharp crease down the front. Finally, the barber unwrapped the towel and patted some Bay Rum on the man's face.

"There you are, Mr. Hays."

From where he sat, Todd could smell the Bay Rum. He wasn't sure he liked that smell on a man. On a woman, yeah, but not on a man. When the well-dressed gent stood, there was something familiar about him, the thin moustache, the fine clothes. It took a moment for Todd to remember where he'd seen him before. It was the gent on the stage, the one who was robbed of his wallet.

Their eyes met as the man walked to the door, but he showed no recognition.

"You're next," the barber said. Todd got in the chair.

"Shave and a haircut?"

"Just a haircut."

"Nice day. Don't take long for that rainy weather to get on a feller's nerves."

"Been raining?"

"All week. Until day before yesterday, then the sun

came out again. Damn country. Snows all winter and rains all summer. Me, I'm going back to Kansas. I'm damned if I'm gonna spend another winter fighting the snow and freezing my ass off."

"You from Kansas?" Todd's interest picked up.

"Yep. Been here a year now, and believe me a year's long enough. Wichita's a good town. More civilized. They've got law and order there. Around here a feller can get shot just for looking straight at somebody, and the law don't care as long as it's working men that shoot each other. Hear about the killing last night? It was some sourdough that lost his dust in the Gold Palace and claimed he was cheated at one of the game tables. He was pitched out and he grabbed his gun. It was an old cap-and-ball pistol fixed to fire rimfire cartridges. But that bouncer shot first. You're a stranger in town, ain't you."

Here was a chance for Todd to ask questions. Barbers, like bartenders, heard everything. "Are there a lot of men from Kansas here?"

"There're men from everywhere, but I've only heard of a few from Kansas. Most Kansans got better sense than to come out here."

Todd watched clipped hair fall from his head in bunches, and he hoped the barber knew what he was doing. The wooden floor creaked as the barber moved from one side of Todd to the other.

"I met a man from Kansas a while back, and I sure would like to meet him again. He told me his name, but I don't remember. He's about my size."

"He owe you some money?"

"Naw. He's just a man I met once."

"About your size, you say?"

"Yeah."

"Could be old Mack. He's from somewhere in Kansas and he's about your size."

"How long's he been here?"

51

"Since last spring. Got a job mucking in the mines, and does a little prospecting when he gets time."

"Oh." Todd was disappointed—again. "He's a working man, huh?"

"Yeah. Working his ass to a frazzle. The smart ones don't work. They just live high on the hog and get rich taking it from the ones that do work. Like old J.D. Hays there. He came here from back east, pitched a big tent, set a plank across two barrels, called it a saloon and started selling whiskey. Now look what he's got. And there's old Babcock. Opened a mercantile, then built a hotel, then got a bank going. Hell, men like that're getting richer and richer without doing a lick of work."

"Oh? Where's Babcock from?"

"Missoura, I think. Who knows." The barber whipped the cloth from around Todd's shoulders, snapped the loose hair from it and said, "Four bits."

A little high-priced, Todd mused, as he stumped down the sidewalk. Bet he didn't charge that much in Wichita. But I reckon that's why he came here, to make money. His hat pushed his ears down now that there wasn't so much hair to hold it up.

"Oh, sir." It was a woman's voice. Todd didn't see where the voice came from, and he paid it no mind. "Oh, sir."

He looked back then, and saw her. She was looking right at him, and only a few feet away. His mouth dropped open, and for a moment he could only stare. She was still the prettiest women he'd ever seen. Wide gray eyes, chestnut hair hanging to her shoulders in curls, slim figure.

"Sir, I wonder if I might have conversation with you."

CHAPTER SIX

Todd Kildow couldn't believe it. "With me?"

"Yes sir. I recognize you. You're the gentleman who scared those robbers away from the stage two days ago."

"Well, uh . . ." He didn't know what to say. Boy, she was pretty.

"If you have a moment, Mr. . . . ?"

He had to think fast to remember. "Brock. Douglas Brock."

"Mr. Brock, I may have a proposition for you."

"Well, sure, ma'am." He was curious as hell, but he waited patiently for her to explain.

"I'm staying at the Palace Hotel. We could talk in the lobby."

"Very well, Miss . . . ?"

She held out her hand to shake. A small feminine hand, white. "I am Miss Leslie Manahan of Bandillo, Texas."

He took her hand in his, but let go quickly, afraid of crushing something so white and soft. "Pleased to make your acquaintance."

"Would you accompany me to my hotel?"

"Yes, ma'am."

Her hotel was the fancy one Todd had backed out of, and when they entered the lobby, the clerk in his

53

coat and ascot gave him a fish eye but said nothing. He removed his hat and waited until she was seated in one of the plush leather chairs, then seated himself in a chair opposite her.

"You're from Texas too, aren't you, Mr. Brock?"

"Yes, ma'am. That is, I've worked in Texas."

"You're a cowboy."

"Most of the time, yes, ma'am."

She smiled. A weak smile, but a pretty one. Clean white teeth. "That was obvious, but even if it weren't I could have guessed. I grew up with cowboys. My father owns the Quarter Circle C. He claims more than a quarter of a million acres."

"That's a big outfit. I think I've heard of it."

"Yes. He has always given us, my younger sister and me, all the advantages. I attended college, in Denver, and my father wanted my sister to attend the same college but . . ." Her voice faltered and she was silent a moment. He could see her gathering determination as she continued. "That's why I'm here, Mr. Brock. My sister ran away from home, and the last letter we received from her was posted here."

She paused again, and again she had to gather herself. "However, I have had no luck finding her. I suspect . . ."

It was hard for her to say whatever she wanted to say, he could see that. He waited. She bit her lower lip and went on.

"Mr. Brock, what I am about to tell you is very personal. It's a personal family matter, but I need help. I know of no one here I can turn to. The marshal said he hasn't seen my sister and doesn't know where to look, except maybe the . . ."

She was a very embarrassed young woman, and had to pause again. He tried to put a sympathetic look on his face. It was easy. He was sympathetic.

54

"You see, Mr. Brock, my sister has a wild streak. Ever since our mother died six years ago she has been, uh, strong-headed and a source of worry to my father. I'm afraid my father is a strict disciplinarian, and my sister rebelled. I need some help locating her, and I was hoping I could . . ." Her voice faltered again. ". . . could trust you. I mean, you look honest, and . . ."

"Sure, Miss Manahan." He spoke softly. "I'll do anything I can."

"I . . . I don't know how to say this. I hope you'll understand. I'll pay you well, of course."

He waited.

"Mr. Brock, being a man, you have no doubt heard of the . . . palaces of pleasure."

"The what?" And then he knew. But he couldn't believe it.

Her face changed. Her mouth tightened, and her expression was hard. "Yes, Mr. Brock, I mean the houses of prostitution."

Still, he couldn't believe it, and he stuttered, "Why . . ."

"I will pay you to go to them and look for my sister."

"You mean . . . your sister . . . ?"

"It's possible, and I have to check out every possibility." She snapped the words. He could tell she was forcing herself to be strictly business. A hard-headed businesswoman. "She should be easy to identify. She inherited our mother's red hair. She's a little shorter than I, and she is beautiful."

Miss Manahan added quickly, "When she wants to be."

Suddenly, her shoulders slumped. She was no longer the businesswoman, just a young woman with a serious problem. "I'm sorry, Mr. Brock. What

I'm asking is extremely extraordinary. Please forgive me." She stood.

"All right," he heard himself say. "If it will help you, Miss Manahan, I'll do it."

She stood, and he stood too, holding his hat in his hands. "You can find me here, Mr. Brock. Do you need some money now?"

"No, you can pay me later."

"Please. Let me give you something now." She opened her bag, and he saw it was the one snatched from her on the stage road. When she handed him a twenty-dollar bill, his eyes widened.

"That's more than enough, Miss Manahan. I don't need this much."

"Please. Just do what you promised. You will, won't you?"

"Yes, ma'am."

"Shoo." He sighed when he was back on the sidewalk alone. The things a man can get into. Palaces of pleasure. Whorehouses. Me.

And getting paid for it.

It was a pretty day, and Todd was restless. No use going to the palaces of pleasure until night. The girls were probably still in bed. Any man who showed up in the daytime would be pitched out on his ear.

The Gold Palace was open for business, and out of curiosity, Todd went in, stepped up to the bar and ordered a beer. Only one gaming table was occupied. The faro and roulette dealers were standing around looking bored. The husky pug who had been standing at the foot of the stairs—the one who had shot and killed a man in the street the night before— wasn't there now. Probably stayed up all night and slept all day, Todd mused.

The beer was cold and good. With only four customers to wait on, the barman, who sported a waxed handlebar moustache, had time on his hands.

"Selling cattle?" he asked.

"No. I just came over here to see what all the excitement is about. I hear men are getting rich around here."

"That they are. The smart ones. And the lucky ones. You doing some prospecting?"

"I'm thinking about it. Trouble is, I don't know how to find gold. I wouldn't know it if it bit me."

A wry smile turned up the barman's mouth under the moustache. "Me neither. If I knew how, I'd be up there digging and scratching with the rest of 'em. I'll bet there's a lot of men up there that don't know what they're doing."

"I'm betting there are men from all over the nation swarming over these hills."

"Just about."

Todd took another swallow of beer. "Good beer. Good and cold. That's something you don't find in Texas. You either drink warm beer or you drink something else."

"You don't find it in Kansas either, where I come from."

"Kansas, you say? I used to know a feller from Kansas. Can't recall his name, but he was about my size."

"I've met a few from Kansas." The barman had to leave and draw more beer for his other customers. Then he got into a conversation with a man in a business suit.

Todd drained his beer mug and banged it down on the bar, hoping to draw the barman's attention. It worked, and he ordered another.

"You say you've met men from Kansas? Do you happen to know anybody about my size? He wouldn't be working for a living. He's kind of a schemer."

"You got a grudge against him?" The barman's

eyes narrowed.

Todd had to lie. "No, I kind of admire the man. Always seems to have money without working his ass off like the rest of us. I'd like to know how he does it."

"There are plenty of schemers around here, but I don't know any from Kansas."

"How does a man do it? I mean how do so many men live without working? I wish I knew."

"Hell, they invest in a business, or they gamble, or they run a whorehouse, or they . . . hell, there's all kinds of ways."

"Yeah." Todd pretended to study the contents of the beer mug. He had taken on a gloomy mood. "Some of them rob and steal and never get caught."

"There's plenty of that going on too."

"Anybody ever get caught around here?"

"Caught?" The barman snorted. "Shot dead." A couple of hardcases tried to rob the bank about a month ago. Huh. That bank's got guards standing around dressed like working men so you wouldn't recognize them. Them two thieves didn't even get back to their horses."

"Was any of them from Kansas?"

Shrugging, the barman said, "Who knows? They were killed in the street. I'd seen one of them in here gambling a lot, but who knows where they were from?" He squinted at Todd. "You're really looking for sombody from Kansas, ain't you."

Todd drained his glass. "Yeah, I thought I might run into him."

"Another beer?"

"Naw. Reckon I'll wander around a while. See what there is to see."

The barman was looking behind Todd, and his expression and voice turned servile. "Yes sir, Mr. Hays. Can I get something for you, sir?"

Todd turned and saw the well-dressed, well-groomed man he'd seen on the stage road and again in the barbershop.

"Bring me a brandy, Bob. I'll be in my office." He turned on his heels and went to the staircase. Todd watched him climb.

"Does he own this place?" he asked. But the barman already had a bottle of brandy and a glass placed on a platter and was carrying the whole thing toward the stairs.

It was a long day. Todd walked down the length of the main street, then to the end of the boardwalk where he found himself on the edge of town. The street forked there, with one fork headed toward the smoke and noise of a sawmill. Todd followed the other fork, wishing he was on horseback instead of walking. After a half-mile it crossed the river. Todd stood on the edge, wondering whether the river could be crossed here any time of the year. It was wide and only about knee deep to a horse, but anybody on foot would sure get wet. How did they do it? Then he saw how.

Two men leading a pack mule came out of the timber on the side. Without hesitation, they took off their boots and pants and waded across, walking gingerly on bare-feet, leading the mule.

"Whew, that's cold," one of them said when his feet touched dry soil.

They looked at Todd, nodded a greeting, and sat in the dirt and put their boots back on. They both had full beards and wore baggy wool pants held up with suspenders. "Know what I'm gonna do?" The other said. "I just hit on a plan to git rich. I'm gonna build a ferry."

He stood and slipped the suspenders over his shoulders. "Yep. Anybody'd pay a dime to ride across this damn river. Hell, they'd pay a quarter."

"Most folks," his partner allowed, "ain't damn

fool enough to be walkin' the way we are. Besides, where you gonna git the money to build anything?"

"Won't take much. I can build a ferry out'n these timbers, and all I'll need is some long cables and two mules on either side to pull the damn thing back and forth."

"Shee-it, if there was any money in it, some dandy would've done it afore now. Somebody like that Babcock or that Hays feller."

"Wa-al, if I don't beat 'em to it, they'll build'er, you see if they don't."

"Shee-it." The first one picked up the pack mule's lead rope and walked away, leading the mule. "If I had a doller for ever' fool idee you git I'd be rich myself."

"If I don't do 'er, sombody else will." He followed his partner toward town.

They weren't out of sight before two men on horseback crossed the river, followed by a man and woman in a buggy. One of the two buggy horses didn't want to get into the water, but the other horse kept it from wheeling and going back, and the man used his long buggy whip enough to convince it that getting its legs wet wasn't all that bad. Todd walked back to the Ponderosa Hotel and was glad to get there and off his feet.

After a short rest, he poured some water from the pitcher into the basin and washed his face. Then he went downstairs again. The little man behind the desk looked at him through wire-framed glasses, but said nothing.

"Fine day," Todd said by way of conversation.

"Humph."

"I hear it's been raining a lot this summer. That's why the grass is so green, I reckon."

"I don't know anything about any grass."

60

"No, I reckon you wouldn't. But that's the first thing a cowman notices wherever he goes."

"Humph."

"Reckon you get people from all over in here. Recollect anybody from Kansas checking in about a year ago? Or maybe it wasn't that long ago."

"We mind our own business."

"Sure, but I thought you might remember a man about my size from Kansas."

The glasses had slipped down on the clerk's nose, and he shoved them back up. "You got a grudge against somebody?"

"No, I met a man from Kansas about a year ago and he said he was thinking about prospecting for gold. I thought he might have stopped here."

"We don't allow no fighting."

"I'm not looking to do any fighting."

"You've been asking questions all over town about somebody from Kansas and you've been to the Gold Palace twice."

"Yeah, well, I would like to find him. That's why I asked you."

"We mind our own business."

"Sure you do."

"Humph."

Another meal in the café. Tasted good. But he didn't hear anything interesting. Back to the Gold Palace for another beer. Four gaming tables were occupied now, but the barman with the handlebar moustache wasn't there. As he drank his beer he looked around for something to do. A man in a flowery vest and with black hair parted in the middle stood behind the faro table. "Care for a game, cowboy?"

"No thanks." He turned back to the bar. It was easy to see how the gamblers fleeced the working men. A

61

man comes to town after being out in the hills or on a trail for months, and he wants to do something besides stand around. It was easy to get him into a game—a game he couldn't win. Todd shook his head when he thought about it. Any time a cowboy, trapper, freighter, or prospector thought he could come to town and beat these slicks at cards, he was just fooling himself and throwing away his money.

He felt, rather than saw, the woman come up behind him. Trying to ignore her, he emptied his beer mug and started to leave.

"See you're still in town, cowboy."

He had to look at her then, and her crooked teeth still ruined her face. "Yep."

"Still looking for a man from Kansas?"

"Yep. About to give up, though."

"Wish I could help you. Buy me a drink and maybe my memory'll work better."

He wondered how she could show so much of her breasts without showing a nipple. "Maybe later. Got to go see a man about a horse."

At the livery barn he found a wooden bench and sat and watched people go by. The livery owner was busy shoveling manure again and didn't say anything. Todd sat there until nearly dark, and went back to the café. His stomach full, he returned to his room, washed his face and combed his hair. Finally, he decided the time had come to begin his search through the palaces of pleasure.

This, he said to his reflection in the mirror, is going to be the damnedest thing I have ever done. He grinned at himself. Yeah, this is something to tell the grandkids about. If I ever have any.

No, on second thought, I don't think I'll tell any kids about this.

CHAPTER SEVEN

As he walked down Pine Street, a block south of Main street, he counted a half-dozen houses with brightly lighted windows and red lanterns hanging on the porches. Whorehouses. The biggest and finest was a wood-frame two-story building with wide bay windows on each side of a wide front door. Lace curtains hung in the two windows. This one was no doubt the most expensive, but he had plenty of money.

Nothing but the best, he grinned to himself as he stepped up on the porch.

His knock was answered almost immediately by a middle-aged woman with red hair, a wrinkled face almost white with talcum powder and a heavy rope of pearls hanging around her neck. Her lowcut dress was the best quality white linen. "Yes?"

"I, uh, I . . ." What did a man say?

Her eyes went over him, stopped at the gun low on his right hip, then went to the boots and spurs. "Have you got money?"

"Yes, ma'am. I can pay."

"You're a little early, but come in." She stepped back and he stepped in. The room was large, with overstuffed chairs and two sofas. The wallpaper was dull red with a white flower design. Two young women lounged on one of the sofas. Two more came in from another room. They smiled at him.

"I'll bet you're in town selling cattle," the middle-aged woman said with a smile.

"Well, uh . . ." He looked over the girls. Every color but red. Only the boss lady had red hair, and she was too old to be the girl he was looking for.

"Care for a drink?"

He didn't really want a drink and he didn't want to pay for one. But how to get out of there? "You see, ma'am, I'm kind of . . ." He grinned sheepishly. ". . . kind of crazy. I like redheads. I'd sure like to find me a redhead."

"Marcia's a redhead. Me too, but I don't play that game anymore." Her head swiveled as her eyes took in the girls. "Where's Marcia?"

"She's comin'," a girl answered, and another girl giggled.

"Comin'? Not yet. Not yet tonight."

"I'll find her." The boss lady left the room.

Todd was very uncomfortable, standing in the middle of the room, holding his hat in his hands. The girls smiled at his embarrassment. They wore satin dresses that came to their knees. A brunette crossed her legs and recrossed them, giving him a view of white thighs. Then the boss lady was back with a girl. A young girl. A girl with red hair.

"Mister, I didn't catch your name."

"Brock. From Texas."

"Mr. Brock, this is Marcia, and she's from Texas too. Aren't you, Marcia?"

"Yeah," the girl said, looking bored. "I know you cowboys."

Another giggle came from the girl on the sofa. "Make him take off his spurs."

The redhead was the right age. A little plump, but

64

girls could gain weight. She could be the Manahan girl. Come to think of it, he didn't know the Manahan girl's first name.

"Would you like to accompany Marcia to her room?"

"Well, uh, yeah."

The girl turned and left, and he followed. She climbed a spiral staircase, and he watched her hips move under the satin dress. She wore no stockings and her feet were encased in dainty slippers. He'd bet she was in demand around White River.

At the second door from the top of the stairs, she went in and closed the door behind them. "That'll be four dollars."

"Expensive, ain't you?"

"In advance. Mrs. Jones said we have to get paid first."

"Can I ask you something?"

"Are you gonna pay me?"

He handed her the twenty, and she went to a dresser, opened the top drawer and brought out a tin box. From that, she counted sixteen dollars and gave it to him.

"She said you're from Texas. Can I ask where in Texas?"

"Fort Worth." She stepped out of the slippers and started unbuttoning the front of her dress.

"Ever been in Bandillo, Texas?"

"Ain't you gonna take off your clothes?"

"Sure. I was just wondering if you know somebody I know."

"Texas is a big place. I don't know everybody there." The dress was down around her waist now, and small, round breasts were exposed. He couldn't help staring. "Come on. We can't take too long."

It just wouldn't do, his mind told him. You're paid

to find her, not go to bed with her. It just wouldn't do. He felt his face getting red as she pushed the dress down to her ankles and stepped out of it. She was naked.

Oh my God. His knees went weak at the sight of her. Why not, his mind asked. You paid for her, and this is her business. Why not? His hands trembled, and a powerful urge came over him. Then he noticed something.

She was not a real redhead.

"You, uh you're no redhead. You dye your hair."

"So what? Don't you like my body?" She turned slowly to give him a good view.

"You're not from Bandillo, Texas."

"I never heard of Bandillo, Texas."

"I . . . gotta go."

"What's the matter? Are you crazy?"

"Yeah, I'm crazy." He yanked the door open and hurried down the stairs. Hurried as fast as a man could with spurs on his boots.

He should have done it, he decided when he was back on the street. He'd paid her, and he was a man with no ties to anybody, and she sure looked good. A little plump, but who cared? On second thought, he might have to look through a half-dozen whorehouses, and he couldn't go to bed with a girl in every one. No man could do that. Not in one night. Huh, he grinned, I could name a lot of men who wouldn't mind trying. If it killed a man, boy, what a way to die.

The second house he went in had no redheads. There were three girls in the parlor, all brunettes, and two men drinking something from small, thick glasses. The madam said they used to have a redhead but the girl had left. "We have some beautiful girls, as you can see," she said.

"What was the redhead's name?"

"Betty, something-or-other. Most don't give their real names anyway."

"What did she look like?"

"Beautiful, of course. There's no call for ugly girls."

"I mean, was she about twenty or twenty-two, and was she from Texas?"

"Are you looking for somebody, mister?"

"Yeah. I am looking for somebody. A girl from Texas."

"Well, maybe she don't want to be found. What are you, a jilted lover?"

"No . . ." He couldn't think of a quick lie.

"I don't know anybody like the one you described, and I don't know as I'd tell you if I did. What a girl does is her own business."

"I apologize for taking up your time. Thanks anyway." He backed out the door.

"You're crazy!" she yelled at him.

Crazy is right, he agreed as he hurried down the walk. This was getting to be a bigger job than he'd expected.

In a saloon named The Buckhorn, or something, he ordered a beer and looked over the crowd. All working men, wearing overalls with suspenders, jackboots, lace-up boots, full beards, moustaches. And women.

"Buy me a drink, cowboy." She was blond and wore the usual low-cut dress. This one was so tight around the hips it looked ready to burst at the seams. In fact, he discovered, one seam on her left hip had split a couple of inches. She wasn't very pretty, but she was the kind that would look good to a man who'd been out in the hills long enough.

"Yeah, all right."

He no more than said it when a bartender was pouring it. As expected, she tossed it down fast with no change of expression.

"Four bits." It was legal robbery, he knew, but he'd expected that too.

"I'm looking for somebody," he said to the girl. "A girl about your age. A redhead. From Texas."

"I don't know any redheads, and besides, I'm from Kansas."

"You are? Did you come out here by yourself?"

She giggled. "Of course not. I came with a man."

"What does he look like?"

"Him? I forgot him already."

"I mean it. I'll buy you another drink if you describe him and tell me where I can find him."

"Oh, George," she said to the bartender. In a few seconds she had another drink swallowed. He paid. "Well, he's about your size and age, and his name was Hooter. That's what everyone called him. I think his last name was Wilson. I heard him called that once."

"You met him in Kansas?"

"No. I met him in Denver about a year ago. He said he was from Kansas too. He talked me into coming up here. Said we could get rich up here. Then he went and got himself killed."

"Oh yeah?" This was getting interesting. "You met him about a year ago, you said? How did he get killed?"

"Trying to rob the bank. Him and another knothead he met. They were shot down in the street."

"Oh, I heard about that. What did he do before he tried to rob the bank?"

"He gambled and robbed a few prospectors. He always wore a rag around his head and changed clothes so nobody would recognize him. The son-of-a-bitch left me with nothing. Listen, I can't just stand here and talk with you without drinking. You know what I mean."

"Oh sure." He reached into his pants pocket.

"We can go to my room out back if you want. It's two dollars."

"Not yet. Maybe later. Let me ask you, did he ever say anything about his past? I mean the robberies and things he'd done?"

Another drink was poured and downed. Todd paid.

"Sure. He bragged about it all the time."

"Did he mention a robbery in western Kansas about a year ago? Three men did some robbing around there and two were killed."

Her brow wrinkled as she tried to remember. "No, I don't recollect him saying anything about a robbery in western Kansas. He was from Kansas City, the Kansas side, and he done some robberies around there. He might have done some more on his way to Denver. He used to brag about how he hadn't done an honest day's work since he was eighteen and he wasn't going to either."

Todd's pulse quickened as he thought it over. Maybe he had found his man. Then his shoulders slumped. The man was dead. A dead man was no help. "Damn," he muttered to himself. "Damn, damn, damn." His right fist balled and he banged it on the bar.

"I'm sorry, mister. Is he the one you was looking for?"

"He could be. Probably is. Was. But how the frozen hell will I ever know?"

"I'm sorry, mister. I really am."

"Here." He handed her two one-dollar bills and left.

69

The plank walk ended a block from the saloon. He stomped on down a dirt path, past whorehouses and more saloons, muttering under his breath.

"Wouldn't you know it? Find the son-of-a-bitch and he's dead. Can't prove a thing by a dead man. All this hunting and asking questions for nothing. The son-of-a-bitch is dead. What now?"

When he realized he was on the outskirts of town, he turned on his heels and went back, still muttering. "What? Go to California and forget everything? Try to make a new life for myself? Give up all my plans for the future?

"What else can a man do?"

By the time he got back to the plank walk he'd made up his mind. Ride out. Wait until daylight, then saddle up and head west. Did that road go on west? Well, he'd find out. Yeah, that's what he'd do.

No, wait a minute. He had somebody else's money in his pocket. He'd promised a lady he'd do a job for her. A promise was a promise. All right, he'd finish the job, do what he'd said he'd do, then ride out.

That decided, his steps quickened, and he headed for the nearest house with a well-lighted front porch.

CHAPTER EIGHT

"A redhead?" the madam asked. "Yes, we have a redhead, but she's busy right now. Why don't you have a drink and wait?" She was fat, motherly looking, but Todd would have bet she was as hard as a rock when she wanted to be.

"If you've got whiskey I'll take a shot."

Wouldn't you know it, the price was four bits, and the whiskey was half water. Two girls with hair the wrong color lounged on a sofa.

"You're from Texas, aren't you? I'll bet you're in the cattle business."

"Yeah. Is the girl, the redhead, from Texas by any chance?"

"You like Texas girls?"

"Sure."

"She's from Texas. I don't know exactly where."

"What's her name?"

"Georgine. We don't ask for surnames here."

"Oh." Maybe. Just maybe.

But when he saw her, his hopes dropped. She was a redhead, but in her thirties with a big bosom and wide hips.

Standing quickly, he said, "Oh, I just remembered something. I've got to go."

"What? Are you crazy?"

71

"Yeah," he said as he yanked open the front door, "I'm crazy."

The next house had only one story, but otherwise it was much the same as the others, and yes, there was a redhead. Todd's hopes picked up. She was young, slender and, except for a crooked nose, right pretty. He reckoned somebody had punched her in the face and broken her nose.

"Three dollars," she said when they were in her room. The narrow bed with an iron bedstead was wrinkled, and when she peeled back the embroidered quilt, he could see a large wet spot on the white sheet.

"Are you from Texas?" No use beating around the bush.

"Texas?" She spoke with a nasal whine. "Do I sound like I'm from Texas? I'm from Saint Louie, and I wish I was back there."

"Excuse me. I just remembered something. I've got to go."

"Go?" Her voice rose. "You haven't paid me. You have to pay me."

He started to reach for the money in his pocket, then changed his mind. Why the hell should he pay her? Hell, she hadn't even taken off her shoes. He opened the door and stepped into the hall.

She was right behind him, yelling in a voice that could have been heard down the street, "Jackson."

Again, "Jackson."

Todd headed for the front door, walking fast, his spurs jangling. He didn't make it.

A short man almost as wide as he was tall appeared in front of the door and blocked his way. The man had a tough square face, dark curly hair showing in his open shirt collar, and a six-gun in his right hand.

"Just hold up there," he said. "What's the trouble?"

72

The motherly type madam stood in the parlor door, hands on hips. The red-headed girl was behind him. "He didn't pay me," the redhead whined.

"Didn't pay you, eh?" The six-gun was a long-barreled Colt .44, and it was aimed at Todd's middle with the hammer back. "You'll pay up, won't you, cowboy?"

Two girls stood behind the madam, watching the show.

"I didn't, uh, do anything," Todd said, looking at the bore of the pistol. "We didn't get on the bed or anything."

"Doesn't matter," the madam answered, her voice hard as granite. "You went to her room, and that means you pay."

"Three bucks," the man said. Big muscles bulged inside his shirtsleeves, and his voice was menacing. "You don't wanta get carried out of here, now, do you, cowboy?"

"Search his pockets, Jackson. Make him pay ten dollars for causing so much trouble."

"You heard the boss. Hand it over. All of it."

Todd hesitated. He'd heard of whorehouses where customers were robbed. No use complaining to the law. The lawdogs would just tell them to stay out of whorehouses and stay out of trouble. He hated to be one of those victims, but he was in no position to argue. The bore of the six-gun could spit instant death, and it didn't waver. They could kill him, dump his body in the alley and forget him. The law would ask questions, but they'd say they never saw him, and that would be the end of that. He reached for his roll of bills, peeled off three ones and handed it to the tough. His jaws were tight and he said nothing as he shoved the rest of the roll back in his pocket.

"Take the rest of it," the women said.

A man appeared from behind the girls, then immediately disappeared. Whoever he was, he wanted no part of this.

"Just stand right still, mister." The gun was still aimed at Todd's middle. The tough's left hand went into his pocket. That was too much. More than a man could stand for and still call himself a man. Todd moved fast.

The explosion from the colt rocked the house, stinging everyone's ears. It meant someone was dying. Or should be.

But the tough, concentrating on searching Todd's pockets, had taken his eyes off Todd's face for an instant. Just an instant. That's all it took for Todd to grab the gun with his left hand and shove the barrel away from his middle toward the parlor door. At the same instant the Remington jumped into his right hand and the bore was against the tough's chest.

For a long moment, no one moved. Todd had taken a desperate gamble, and for a couple of seconds he couldn't believe it had worked. He should be lying on the floor with a .44 slug in his gut. But it had worked, and the short man saw death coming his way. He stood perfectly still, looking down at the Remington, breathing in quick, shallow breaths. His hold on the Colt loosened. Out of the corner of his eye, Todd saw the madam on her side on the floor, holding her left arm. Blood oozed between her fingers.

An awful silence fell over the house.

Then the madam groaned and sat up, and one of the girls screamed. Another joined in.

Blinking back his surprise, Todd gathered his wits. He twisted the Colt out of the tough's hand and spoke in a hissing tone. "Through the door. We're going outside." He moved the bore of the Remington up under the tough's nose.

"Wha . . . what're you gonna do mister?" The tough stood ramrod-straight. Only his lips moved.

Barely moving his own lips, Todd said, "I don't know. Blow your head off, maybe. Depends on how you behave. Walk slow, but walk. Turn around and go through that door. Now."

Turning slowly, the short man opened the door and stepped out onto the porch. Lantern lights showed cold fear in his face. Todd followed, then ordered the man to turn around. While the tough watched, Todd holstered the Remington and took the long-barreled Colt in his right hand.

"What're you gonna do?"

Instead of answering, Todd whipped the gun up, and the long barrel collided with a loud smack against the side of the man's face. The man pitched sideways, and Todd followed, hitting him again.

The door was filled with girls, watching. A scream came from one of them. Two of them screamed. Their bodyguard was down on the wooden porch, holding his face in his hands. Todd stood over him.

"I'm not going to kill you," he hissed, "but you tried to rob me and I hate robbers. I hate thieves and robbers more than I hate anything." With that, he swung the Colt again and heard it smack the side of the man's head. He swung it again.

Then, after the tough was out cold, he stepped off the porch, threw the Colt into some bushes beside the porch, and walked away.

Now that it was over, he felt weak. His hands were shaking and his knees weren't very steady either. It was a familiar feeling. It had come to him in the war, in western Kansas and in Santa Fe. Good Lord, he thought, I'm no fighter. That scared the pure hell out of me. Lord, but I'm lucky to be alive!

Looking back over his shoulder, he saw three of the girls helping their bodyguard to his feet. He staggered, and all four of them nearly went down. Next, the madam came out with a girl on each side of her, helping her. She gripped her left arm as they came down the steps and walked slowly, carefully to the street. Were they going to the law? No, Todd decided as he watched from a dark spot under a tall ponderosa. They were going to a doctor somewhere.

Just to be sure, he watched them, staying in the dark. They went a block down that street, turned a corner and went up to a two-story stone house. He followed until he was close enough to see a sign over the porch, announcing that this was the home of Richard Hall, M.D.

They wouldn't go to the law. They wanted no more to do with the law than he did. The bullet wound was the result of an accident, they would say.

Relieved, Todd turned toward Main Street. How many whorehouses had he been in that night? He'd lost count. There were more, but for a while he needed a breather. He'd have a beer at the Gold Palace, then finish the chore.

The big room was packed. Three bartenders were pouring drinks as fast as they could work. All the gaming tables were occupied, and the roulette wheel was turning. Men's voices were so loud Todd had to yell at a bartender to order a beer. When the roulette wheel stopped, someone let out a "Whoo-haw, she's a winner, boys," and a crowd quickly gathered at the roulette table.

His glass drained, Todd tried to order another, but couldn't get a bartender's attention. "Hell with it," he muttered, and left.

He reckoned it was about ten o'clock now, too early to go to bed, but getting late for a cowboy from the hills.

The evening had just begun in White River, however. Whorehouse row was lively with men coming and going. Todd approached a house, saw through the window that four men were sitting in the parlor, and backed away. Bad enough to have to go in and ask his questions without having a bunch of men listening.

He had started up the path to another house when he met a man coming out. The man was muttering every four-letter word Todd had ever heard. "God-damned thieves. Son-of-bitchin' bunch of pick-pockets." He spotted Todd and said, "Don't go in there, mister. They got creepers in there."

"What? Creepers?"

"Yeah, They'll steal ever'thing you got."

"Creepers?"

"Shore. Don't you know nothin'? Where you from, anyhow?"

"Texas."

"You don't know nothin' then. Wa-al, I'll tell you somethin'. Listen to me and learn." The man pulled a plug of tobacco out of a shirt pocket and bit off a hunk. He chewed hurriedly intil he had enough juice to spit a stream onto the path. "What they do is, they wait till you get buck nekked on the bed with a girl, then they sneak in and take ever'thing out of your pockets. You don't hear 'em come in, and even if you do you can't chase 'em buck nekked that way."

"And," Todd finished the story for him, "I'm guessing that if you complain they've got a tough son-of-a-bitch with a gun and a billy club to shut you up."

"You're not so dumb after all." He squirted

77

another brown stream on the path. "They shore as hell do, and they'll kill you and throw your carcass in the river. Best don't go in there."

"All right, friend, I'll take your advice. Much obliged." Todd turned to go.

"You're from Texas, you say? I'm from Arkansaw. I got a little claim 'bout ten mile up the river, and I been a-diggin' up a little color. Right now, I'm plumb busted, howesomever. They took it all in there."

Shaking his head sadly, Todd started down the path.

"I was a-goin' over to the Gold Palace and get a drink of whiskey, but now I'm plumb busted."

"Come on," Todd said, "I'll stand for a shot of whiskey."

The room was still crowded and noisy and the bartenders were still busy. They elbowed their way to the bar and tried to order a drink. For a full ten minutes, they were ignored, then finally a bartender came over.

"What'll it be?"

"You call it," Todd said to the man from Arkansas.

"Whiskey. The ranker the better."

"Two."

Neither man spoke until the whiskey was delivered, paid for, and the Arkansan had swallowed his in a gulp. "Whee," he said. "Shoo," Todd said after he'd taken a sip. "That'll make you slap mosquitoes where there ain't any."

"It'll make a rabbit rear up on its hind legs and fight a bear."

"You found some gold, you say?"

"Yup. Got 'er staked out legal. She's a good 'un."

"You're lucky. I heard most men don't find anything but granite."

"Most don't. But it wasn't all luck. I dug a lot of

78

holes for a lot of years before I hit'er. You prospectin'?"

"Naw. I came here looking for somebody, a gent from Kansas. I think I found him, but he's dead."

"He a pal?"

"Naw. Just somebody I wanted to meet."

"That's tough. Air you a-goin' back to Texas now?"

Rubbing his jaw, Todd said, "Naw. Not yet. Now I'm looking for somebody else. A girl. A redhaired girl."

"Tell you what, if you'll buy another'n, I'll git back to town in a few days and buy you whiskey till it comes out your ears. Shit, I don't wanta go back to my diggin's without a hangover."

"I'll buy."

The Arkansan nodded his approval, and said, "It's none of my business, but how come you're lookin' fer a girl?" Then he added quickly, "Don't tell me if you don't want to."

Todd mulled it over while more whiskey was delivered and tasted. This time the Arkansan sipped his slowly. Why not tell him? He didn't have to mention names. He told him.

"Uh-huh. That's why you was a-goin' to that cathouse."

When Todd said nothing further, he went on, "Wa-al, I know a red-headed girl. Know of 'er. How old a girl air you a-lookin' fer?"

"Around twenty, maybe twenty-two."

"Hmm." The Arkansan took another sip. "Could be her. Ain't rich, howesomever. She's a diggin' and a-scratchin', but she don't know what she's a-doin' and she ain't about to strike'er."

"You know a girl who's prospecting? A red-haired girl?"

"Yep. Know right whar she is. Livin' alone in a log

79

shack, and carries a new Winchester repeatin' rifle ever'whar she goes. Knows how to shoot it to."

"A young girl?"

"Yep. Might be purty if she wanted to be. The kind of clothes she wears don't show it, but I'll bet she's got a good figger."

"From Texas?"

"Wa-al now, I don't know whar she's from. Fact is, I don't know nothin' about 'er 'cept she's got red hair and she's a-livin' alone."

"I wonder . . . Tell me where to find her." He couldn't picture a girl from a wealthy Texas ranch family living alone in a mountain cabin and digging for gold, but it was something he'd have to report to Leslie Manahan.

CHAPTER NINE

The clerk behind the desk at the Palace Hotel shot a scowl at him the second he walked in the door. That rankled Todd. Sure, he wore a working cowboy's clothes, but they weren't too dirty. Sure, he had spurs on his boots, but he spent a lot more time on horseback than on foot. And the Remington, hell, nearly everybody carried a gun of some kind.

"I'm here to see Miss Leslie Manahan," he said. "Which room is she in?"

"Your name?" Todd gave the name of Douglas Brock. "You wait here and I'll go up and ask her if she wants to see you."

The clerk left his long desk and climbed the spiral staircase. Todd took a seat in one of the leather chairs in the lobby. In a few minutes the clerk came down and went through a connecting door into the hotel's restaurant. When he came back he said, "Miss Manahan is taking breakfast, sir. She asked if you would care to join her." He said "sir" with a sneer.

Todd stood and headed for the connecting door. He felt like saying something sarcastic to the clerk, but nothing came to mind. Leslie Manahan waved to him, and he no more than approached the table where she was sitting alone when she blurted out, "Did you find her?" Before he could answer, she

81

added, "Please excuse my manners, Mr. Brock. Won't you sit down? May I order you some breakfast?" She was trying to be calm, he could tell, but she was biting off the words.

The table was covered with a white linen cloth, and the silverware looked like silver. The young woman, with her long auburn curls and wide gray eyes, was still the prettiest woman he'd ever seen. "No thanks, Miss Manahan I've had breakfast." He pulled out a chair and sat.

"Would you like some coffee, then?"

"Yes, if you please. Coffee would be fine."

A waiter in a white coat must have been listening because he was right there with a coffeepot and a china cup and saucer. They didn't speak until he left. Then she said, "I'm afraid to ask, but did you find her?"

"No. I tried. I asked a lot of questions. But I didn't find anybody who looks the way you described your sister."

A sigh from her. "It's a relief. As badly as I want to find her, I'm happy to know that she . . ." Miss Manahan didn't finish what she'd started to say.

"It's possible that she's no longer in White River, Miss Manahan."

"Yes. That's possible." She stared at he china plate and the remains of eggs and bacon. "I really don't know where to look next."

Todd shifted in his chair and cleared his throat. He knew that what he was about to say was none of his business, but he believed it ought to be said. "Uh, Miss Manahan, maybe I shouldn't say this, but could it be that she doesn't want to be found?"

"Yes, that's another possibility. My father and I considered that. But I had to try."

"What will you do now?" He sipped the coffee. It was strong and good.

"Go back to Denver and wire my father. I'm hoping that Marietta has contacted him since I left home." Her gray eyes were sad. "Right now that's the only thing I can think of to do."

Todd reached into his pocket, pulled out his roll of bills and peeled off ten. "Here. This is what's left of your twenty."

"Oh, I expected you to spend that, and I want to pay you more. Would another ten dollars be enough?"

"Oh no. I can't take your money."

"Of course you can. My father is quite wealthy, and you've earned it."

He couldn't help grinning when he thought about what he'd done to earn it and what he could have done, but he wiped the grin off his face immediately. He hoped she didn't see it. "I did hear of a red-haired girl who is living alone in a cabin and prospecting for gold. The man who described her said she's young, but that's all he knows about her."

Leslie Manahan's head came up. "Where?"

"He told me where to find her. It's about ten miles northwest, across the river."

"Will you go there and see her, Mr. Brock? I'll pay you, of course."

"The way he described her, she's not likely to be your sister."

"It's just a small chance, of course, but I have to be sure. Will you do that?"

"All right. You said Marietta. Is that her name?"

"Yes. You have a horse, do you not?"

"Sure. Two of them."

"Will you do that for me?"

"Yes, ma'am. I'll start right now."

He left the pack horse behind and rode the young

83

bay. It was good to be on horseback again. It made a man feel bigger, taller somehow. Superior to a man on foot. The bay didn't want to wade across the river, so Todd treated it the way he'd treat any green colt. Anticipating when the horse would try to spin away, he rode it as close as it would go, then stopped and made it stand there and look at the water. After a long minute, he turned the horse around, rode in a big circle and came back and did the same thing. Each time the horse went a little closer. It took three tries to get it into the water, and then it splashed across the river hurriedly.

Todd had always prided himself at being a good hand with young horses. He liked colts. He also liked cattle and being a cowboy. Raised on a farm in eastern Kansas, he'd done his share of plowing, cultivating, harvesting, and milking cows, but his ambition was to be a cattleman. When his folks sold their farm and moved west to take advantage of free land, he saw his chance. The war slowed him down, but when the war ended he homesteaded his own quarter-section on the edge of the public domain where he could graze cattle free.

He bought forty long horn cows and some bulls out of a trail herd going through from the Indian Nation. The next year he'd bought forty more. The winters were mild and he had a seventy-five percent calf crop, good for range cattle. He was on his way to realizing his ambition.

Then he found his folks murdered, and that ruined everything.

Now as he rode west on a wagon road in Colorado Territory, he brought his mind back to the present. Let's see, follow the river west until he came to the second creek from the north. Follow the second creek that emptied into the river—for about four miles—

84

and he ought to see the cabin.

It was another rocky mountain road, nothing but two wagon tracks. At places it left the river to wind through the timber and buckbrush. He crossed a narrow creek that came from the north and kept going until he came to another creek. It too joined the river from the north. A barely visible trail led north on the side of a hill, cut through two acres of buck brush and continued along the creek. Realizing how easy it would be to get lost in the mountains, Todd stopped now and then and took a good look behind him, trying to pick out landmarks.

He crossed a green valley full of wildflowers and tall grass and followed the path into the timber again. Twice, he crossed the creek and continued north. At one place, out in the open, there was a string of four beaver ponds in the creek, but the beaver dams looked old. The pointed, chipped stumps of aspen told him the trees had been cut down by beaver, but they too were old. There were no tracks on the path. No one had traveled on it since the last hard rain. When he came out of the timber he saw the cabin.

It was one room, barely big enough for a bed and stove. It was made of logs chinked with mud from the creek. Wind and rain had eroded the mud in places,leaving gaps between the logs. The roof was tarpaper.

Remembering that the girl was armed with a Winchester, he approached slowly, eyes taking in everything. A dun horse was picketed with a long rope behind the cabin, and that was the only living creature he saw. But where there was a horse on a picket there had to be a man or a girl. Somebody.

"Hello-o-o," he yelled, reining up. No answer. "Hello-o-o."

He rode closer. Small rocks were piled near the cabin door, and he guessed that somebody had examined them for a sign of gold. A pick and two shovels, one with a round point and one with a square point, leaned against the cabin on the other side of the door.

"Hello-o-o."

After a minute, he rode around the cabin, then turned back to the creek and rode upstream. There was more buckbrush and a clearing. That's where he saw her.

She was no soldier, he could tell at a glance. Her back was to him and she didn't see him as she stood knee-deep in the creek. The legs of her denim overalls were rolled up, but not high enough to stay dry. She had a flat pan in her hands, studying its contents.

A lever-action rifle lay on the grassy bank a good forty feet from her. She carried no other gun that he could see. A soldier wouldn't get that far from his weapon.

Todd sat his horse, trying to decide whether to holler and get her attention or ride up and get between her and the rifle. She could be dangerous. A young woman living alone in a mountain cabin had to be a little touched in the head. If she got her hands on that gun she might shoot first and then ask what he wanted.

The horse's hoofbeats were almost soundless on the grassy meadow, and the rolling creek drowned out what little sound they made. He rode up between her and the rifle and sat there, watching. She was red-haired, all right, and young. Her baggy bib overalls were held up with denim suspenders, and her checkered shirt was about two sizes too big. So was her high-crown floppy hat. A wisp of red hair hung down one side of her face, and tendrils on the back of her neck were red.

She emptied the pan and used it to scoop more sand and gravel from the creek bottom. She moved the pan slowly in a circular motion, studying the contents intently.

"Hell," he said softly, still on his horse. It would have been bad manners to dismount without being invited to. She didn't hear above the swirling sound of the water.

"Hello," he said again, louder.

She glanced his way, then straightened up as if she'd been kicked in the seat. Her eyes were wild and her mouth opened and closed. For a moment, they looked at each other. Todd wanted to say something to let her know he was harmless, and finally he said conversationally, "Purty day. Finding anything?"

"Who are you? What do you want?" Her eyes went to the rifle on the grass behind him, then back to his face. She had green eyes, not gray like Miss Leslie Manahan, and she was about two inches shorter, though not stubby short.

What to say? And how to say it? Just ask her name? Maybe she wouldn't tell him. If she was Miss Manahan's sister, maybe she wouldn't admit it. Be blunt?

Before he knew what he was saying, the words came out, accusing. "You are Marietta Manahan."

"What? Who are you?"

"Your sister, Miss Leslie Manahan, hired me to find you."

"My sister? She's here?"

The response surprised him. She really was Marietta Manahan. She as much as admitted it. He swallowed his surprise.

"Yes, ma'am."

"Leslie? Is here?"

87

Now he was sure. "Yes, ma'am. She's staying in White River and she's traveled a long ways to see you."

The girl waded out of the creek. She was barefoot and he wondered how she could stand the cold water. He made no move when she picked up the rifle and cocked the hammer back. In her baggy clothes, she could have been mistaken at a distance for a man, but there was no mistaking the smooth face, the slender neck and wrists, and the small hands. Callused hands with broken fingernails, but feminine hands.

She didn't point the gun at him, but she kept her finger on the trigger, ready. "Where did you meet my sister?"

"In White River. She needed help finding you and she hired me."

"Who are you?"

"My name is T . . ." He almost let it slip. "Douglas Brock. I'm from Texas too."

"You're a drifter." It was an accusation.

"Yess, ma'am, that's what I am."

Her eyes took in the Remington. "And you're a gunfighter."

"Not unless I have to be."

For another long moment, she studied his face. He sat his horse easily, holding its head up to keep it from reaching the grass. Then she said, "All right Mr. Douglas Brock, I want you to do two things. I want you to turn around and go right back to White River. And I want you to tell my sister that I am well and healthy and I am not going home."

Shrugging, he said, "Whatever you say, ma'am. It's no skin off my nose." He reined the bay back the way he'd come, then stopped. "But if I'm any judge of people, you either go to town and see your sister or she'll come here to see you." Touching spurs to the bay, he started on.

"Wait."

He stopped and looked back.

"All right. I'll get my horse and go back with you."

"Fine. But would you mind letting the hammer down on that rifle? It might go off."

CHAPTER TEN

Todd Kildow was never much of a talker. His mother and other relatives had often described him as a quiet boy. But he had never ridden side by side with anyone for as long as an hour without saying something. Not until now. She kept her horse in the left wagon track and he stayed on the right, and she made it clear right from the beginning that she didn't consider this a social occasion. Her loose-fitting overall legs crawled up with the motion of the horse, exposing a man's socks over a man's lace-up, high-top shoes. A boy's shoes, rather.

Well, if she didn't want to talk, that was all right with him.

At the river, his horse balked again, and again he rode it around in a big circle. Then it saw her horse in the water and followed. She stopped in the middle of the river, watching him handle the bay, but still she said nothing.

Not until they had ridden down Main Street and stopped in front of the Palace Hotel, did he speak. "She's in there, probably. Want me to take your horse to the livery barn?"

Dismounting, she answered, "No. He'll stand tied." She wrapped the reins around a hitchrail, and stepped onto the plank walk. He watched her while she looked down at herself, looked up and down the street, squared her shoulders and walked with determined steps into the hotel.

That was that. His job was done. What happened between the two sisters was none of his business. One of them did owe him a couple of dollars, and he could use the money, but he wasn't about to go in there and ask for it.

What now? Ride on? No reason to stay around here. At the livery barn, he off-saddled the bay and put him in the pen with his pack horse. He carried a double armload of hay to them and pumped a tub full of water. Let them rest another day, and tomorrow he'd put them to work climbing mountains again. His stomach and a glance at the sky told him it was mid-afternoon and he hadn't had dinner. He went to the cafe where he'd been before, and found only one of the tables occupied and no one sitting at the counter.

"Hope you can find something for me to eat," he said to the middle-aged woman behind the counter.

She grumbled, "Dinner was over two hours ago, but I'll see if I can find something."

"Anything will do."

"Yeah," she mumbled as she went to the kitchen, "that's the only good thing about you cowboys, you'll eat anything."

His meal was a slice of cold beef between two thick slices of bread, and though she didn't know it, it was delicious to him. "I'll be back for supper," he said as he paid.

"Yeah, don't wait too long."

At the Ponderosa Hotel, the clerk scowled at him over the wire-rim glasses and groused, "You didn't pay for three nights. If you don't pay me now I'll lock your stuff up."

"I knew you were gonna say that." Todd grinned in spite of himself. He reached for the roll of bills in his pocket. "Here, this'll pay for tonight. I'll be gone early in the morning."

"Don't take no towels or blankets or anything with you, and be quiet when you leave. We don't allow no noise in here."

"I knew you were gonna say that too."

In his room, he pulled off his boots and flopped down on the feather bed. A man could get used to a bed like that. But he'd better not. He lay on his back with his hands under his head, sighing contentedly. A man had to take his comforts where he could and when he could. No telling when he'd sleep in a bed again. Another sigh came from him.

His bed back home was filled with cotton, not feathers, but it was better than sleeping on the ground. He had a good place. His house was one room made of rough lumber, but it was a big room and it had a wooden floor. A two-lid stove with an oven was all he needed for the cooking he did. When he got hungry for a woman-cooked meal he called on his folks only three miles away. They had chickens and hogs and they raised some corn and spuds, and they had plenty to eat. He didn't care much for the farming, but he had to cultivate some land to prove up on his claim, so he grew oats and hay for his horses and cattle. Most of the time the cattle were able to forage for themselves, but he'd been warned that every few years or so a hard snowstorm hit that part of the country and a stockman had better be prepared. He ate a lot of wild meat—dear, antelope, turkeys, geese.

Yeah, things were going well, and he'd started looking around for a woman. A man needed a woman. Then . . .

"Aw hell." He groaned and turned over on his side.

He'd found his dad's body out by the barn, a bullet through the heart. His mother lay in a mess of blood on the floor in the kitchen, a bullet in her forehead. She'd looked up the bore of the gun and seen it coming. Thank God she'd died instantly. The money they'd kept in a jar in a cabinet over the kitchen pump was gone. Two loaves of fresh-baked bread sat on the kitchen table. She'd always baked more than two loaves. And when he'd run back outside, horrified, he saw that the black mare was gone too.

His first thought was to ride for town as hard as his horse could run. Get the sheriff. Get some townsmen and go after them. But town was ten miles away, and the killers had gone in the opposite direction. Their trail was easy to follow. Four horses, including the black mare. Half crying, half crazy with anger, he'd chased after them.

"Oh God," he groaned. "God, oh God. Why can't a man forget?"

An hour later, he got up, washed his face and sat on the edge of the bed. He had to forget it. They were dead. Two of the killers he had killed himself, and now the third had been shot to death trying to rob a bank. Too bad. He'd hoped that by some miracle he'd find the third man and force a confession out of him. But that was hoping for too much. He'd been trying to convince himself there was hope. Now there was none. Might as well drift on.

Unless . . .

Why didn't he think of it before? That man, Hooter Wilson or whatever his name was, liked to brag. His woman—his ex-woman—mentioned that he liked to brag about his crimes. He's probably told somebody about killing a farm couple in western Kansas and surviving an ambush. Or, if he didn't talk about the murders, he'd at least have bragged about surviving an ambush. He'd have exaggerated a little, had it a whole sheriff's posse instead of only one man, but he'd have told somebody about it. The woman? Maybe. Just maybe.

His face washed and his hair combed, he put his hat on—still didn't like the feel of it now that he had a haircut—and went out on the street. It was late afternoon. Traffic was heavy. A steam whistle signaled a shift change for workers in a mine on the outskirts of town. Men were pouring into the Gold Palace in droves. Todd walked past the Gold Palace, turned the corner and went into the Buckhorn Bar. He saw the blond woman in the low-cut dress between two miners, pouring a shot of liquor—or something—down her throat. He took his time drinking the mug of beer a bartender brought, hoping for a chance to talk to the woman. He wished he knew her name. After three beers, he gave up. He'd try again later that night.

Horses cared for, he went back to the café, thinking he'd better not be late for supper. The place was packed. Every seat at the counter was filled. So were the half-dozen wooden tables. The middle-aged waitress had a younger woman helping her, but still both women were hurrying as fast as their feet could move without running. Todd turned to leave, then saw two people he didn't expect to see. They were sitting at a table for four, waiting for service. One spotted him and waved him over.

It was the Manahan sisters.

When he took a better look he saw why they were

here instead of in the Palace Hotel's dining room. Marietta, the red-haired one, was still wearing her baggy overalls, and Leslie, the older one, was now wearing a long-sleeved broadcloth shirt, a divided riding skirt and boots. The Palace would frown on that kind of clothing.

"Mr. Brock, won't you join us." It was the older one speaking. "I want to pay you for your help." Damn, she was pretty.

Even so, he really didn't want to join them. He didn't know how to make small talk with a lady. But he didn't know how to decline. "Are you sure you won't mind? I don't want to intrude."

"We'll be happy to have you, won't we Marrie?"

The redhead's green eyes met Todd's pale blue ones for a moment. "Yeh," she said.

Todd sat down, but didn't know what to talk about.

"I want to pay you right now before you get away from us." Leslie Manahan reached inside her pocketbook, produced a ten-dollar bill and handed it to Todd. He put it in his shirt pocket.

"Thank you. I was glad to help."

"You don't know how much you helped me, Mr. Brock. We—my father and I—would have been worried sick if you hadn't found Marrie for us."

Todd stood. "It was a pleasure working for you, Miss Manahan. If there's anything else I can do, holler."

"My name is Leslie. Or Les. No one at the ranch calls me Miss Manahan. No one. And, yes, there is one more thing you can do. Please, sit."

He sat again, puzzled.

Leaning back in her chair, she looked at her younger sister and at Todd. "What you can do, Douglas—may I call you Douglas?—what you can do is try to talk some sense into my sister." Before he could say anything, she went on, "She refuses to go home. All right, I can understand, and I won't quarrel about it anymore. But..." She paused. Todd was uncomfortable.

"I wish you would tell her about the dangers of staying alone in a town like White River. Tell her how dangerous it is to live alone in a cabin in the mountains. Tell her about the stage robbery, what almost happened to me, and about all the other robberies around here." She was looking directly at Todd. The red-haired one was watching him too, a slightly amused expression on her face.

Todd felt himself getting red. This was no place for him. Clearing his throat, he said, finally, "It is true. I've heard of prospectors being robbed. If I lived alone in the hills, I'd keep a gun within reach all the time, and I'd keep my eyes peeled. In fact, I'd almost be afraid to sleep in a cabin. Too easy for somebody to sneak up on you." There. He'd said what Miss Manahan wanted him to say. Now maybe he could excuse himself. No such luck.

The redhead definitely was amused. "What would you do when it rains, Doug? Couldn't you barricade the door some way so no one could break in without waking you up?"

"Is that what you do, Marrie?" It was her sister asking.

Marietta Manahan didn't take her eyes off Todd's face. "And do you think a bravo man can shoot better than a woman?"

Now she was getting sarcastic. And that half-smile was irritating. "Maybe yes, maybe no. But it was awful easy to get between you and your gun up there. I could have made off with your gun, horse and everything."

97

That did it. The amused expression left her face. "You're right. I won't let that happen again. I'm going to get a revolver and carry it in a holster low, the way you do."

Leslie Manahan groaned. "Oh no. You're determined to go back and live like a hermit."

"Yup," the redhead said. "I can do anything a man can do. As soon as we get something to eat, I'm going to the Gold Palace and have a drink of whiskey."

"Oh no. Marrie, I've seen you do some crazy things, but I never thought you'd habituate a saloon. And drink whiskey?"

"Wanta go with me?"

"Of course not."

"Why? Scared?"

"You bet I'm scared."

"Of what? Doing something on your own? Doing something that D . . . tradition wouldn't approve of?"

Now he understood. Maybe. She was showing off. Being wildly different just to show her sister she wasn't afraid to. Doing something her dad would get madder than hell about, just to spite everybody. Well, it wasn't any of his business, and he wished he could find a way to excuse himself.

"Doug?" the gray eyes were turned to him. "Have you ever heard of anything so outlandish?"

"Have you, Doug?" Now it was the green eyes. "You've seen women in saloons, haven't you?"

"All right. I'll go." The gray eyes were determined. "We'll find out who's scared."

"Good. As soon as we get the wrinkles out of our bellies."

Now he could leave. This whole thing was between two sisters. He tried to think of a reason for leaving. Too late. The middle-aged waitress was there.

Leslie Manahan ordered first. "I'd like the roast beef, please, and mashed potatoes and gravy."

"Same here," said the red-haired one.

"And you, mister?"

"Oh, same here."

Damn. He was stuck.

While they waited, the two girls talked about their dad and the Quarter Circle C Ranch. The older one broke the news about Mister Manahan running for Congress, but the younger one wasn't surprised. In fact, she smiled a wicked smile.

"It's for sure he doesn't want me at home. I'm a family disgrace."

"He wants you at home, and he wants you to behave yourself."

"Sure. He wants me to be the perfect lady and marry some spoiled rich bastard."

"Dad loves you, Marrie. Why do you hate him?"

The wicked smile was gone now. "I don't hate him, Les. It's just that I don't want to live under his domination."

Todd squirmed uncomfortably in his chair. This was something he shouldn't he hearing.

"All right, you're twenty-one, and you can do as you please. But we wish you would live in a city where a young woman alone isn't so . . . so vulnerable. You could find a good man. He doesn't have to be rich."

"I'll never again live under anyone's domination."

Thank God the meal came, and he could busy himself eating.

CHAPTER ELEVEN

It was peach cobbler again for dessert. They all cleaned their platters. The Manahan sisters had healthy appetites. especially the red-haired one. She ate like a man. And the older one was acting and talking like a ranch woman.

When they were presented with the price, Todd offered to pay the whole bill, but they wouldn't have it and he was glad of it. Excusing himself wasn't a easy as he'd hoped, however.

"What are your plans, Doug?"

"Plans? I don't have any. Except to stick around here another day or two."

"Good. Then maybe we'll see you again. I hope we do."

"Yes. That would be nice." He realized he'd talked like a sissy gentleman, but he didn't know what else to say. Finally, he excused himself and left. He didn't give a reason, and they didn't ask.

"Shoo." It was good to be outside. He inhaled deeply and got a lungful of smoke from one of the steam engines that ran a mine hoist. Coughing, he wondered how people in the mining towns and the cities kept from getting consumption. Too many people could sure mess things up.

After having supper with the Manahan sisters, the

last person he wanted to talk to right away was another woman. But he needed information. Damn, he said to himself as he started walking, why can't it be a man I have to ask questions of instead of another woman?

Wagon traffic on the street was lighter now, but foot traffic was heavy on the sidewalks. Boots thumping and spurs ringing, Todd strode past the Palace Hotel, the Gold Palace, around the corner and into the Buckhorn saloon. This time, she saw him before he saw her, and she came over.

"Evenin', cowboy. I see you're still in town. Buy me a drink?" She put her hand through his left arm. Until he'd met Leslie Manahan, this one might have looked tolerable, but not now. She didn't even belong in the same race as Leslie Manahan.

"Sure. I was looking for you anyway." He ordered a beer and the bartender knew what to serve her. It looked like whiskey, but she snatched it as soon as it was poured and tossed it down her throat. She said, "Aahh," and blinked a couple of times.

"You wanted to see me? Wanta go out back?"

"No, I just want to ask you something."

"Ask me something? What?"

"That man you came here with, what did you say his name was? Hooter? He sounds like the man I was looking for. I . . ."

She cut him off. "Listen, if you want to ask me about Hooter, we'd better go out back. The boss doesn't like for me to stand here talking with one man too long. It's two dollars."

Did he want to go out back with her? No, he decided. But he did want some answers, and if it cost two dollars it would be worth it. He finished his beer in three quick swallows. "All right. Let's go."

"You have to pay now." He handed her two dollars

which she turned over to the bartender. Then she led the way and he followed, watching her hips move inside the sheath dress. No, she didn't come close to Leslie Manahan.

The wind had shifted, and the air outside tasted good after the smoke in the saloon, but he got to take only a few breaths before she stepped in front of a one-room shack, opened the door and went inside. There, she lit a coal oil lamp and closed the door behind him. Without another word she stepped out of her slippers, stripped off the dress and stood before him in nothing but her underpants. Her breasts were big and heavy and her thighs were thick.

"Don't you wanta get naked too?"

He couldn't take his eyes off her. "No, all I want is some answers." So she wasn't beautiful. She was female. "Did Hooter ever mention murdering a farm couple in western Kansas?"

Bending to pull down the coverlet on the bed, she looked over her shoulder at him. He had an urge to put his hands on her buttocks. "Why do you keep askin' about Hooter? The son-of-a-bitch is gone and by God forgotten."

"I'm looking for a man who killed some people in Kansas and he might be the one. If he is, he was with two other men at the time. About a year ago."

Straightening, she hooked her thumbs in the top of her underpants and prepared to pull them down. "He didn't say nothin' about it to me. Why don't you ask his other woman."

"His other woman?"

"Yeah. One woman wasn't enough for the son-of-a-bitch. He was sneaking around with that Lilly at the Gold Palace."

"Did he ever talk about escaping from an ambush? The three men were ambushed one night and the other two were killed. He got away. Did he ever mention that?"

"Not to me. Do you want to get down to business or don't you? We haven't got all night." Leslie Manahan, she wasn't.

"No," he suddenly decided. "I'll pass. Thanks, anyway." He went to the door.

"What are you, crazy?" The last thing he heard her say was, "You're crazy."

Damn. This was getting nowhere. Lilly? Is that what she said the other woman's name was? Yeah, Lilly. In the Gold Palace. Wouldn't you know it? Since he'd left Texas last spring, he'd met two kinds of women. There was Leslie Manahan, very proper and ladylike and there were the whores. Make that three kinds. There was Marietta Manahan, somewhere in between. He was sick of the whores, and Leslie Manahan was out of his reach. Or was she?

She did show an interest in him and said she wanted to see him again. It couldn't be because she had another job for him. Boy, she's some woman. Talked like a lady, but only when she thought she ought to. Sounded like a ranch woman the rest of the time.

Some woman.

But naw. She thought of him the way she thought of a hired cowboy. Honest, dependable, but a hired man just the same. Forget it, Todd Kildow, he told himself. Go hunt up this Lilly. Yeah, go to the Gold Palace and try to get information out of another whore.

Inside, the noise was almost painful to the ears.

Men's laughter, yells and cursing. The game tables were all filled. At the bar, men stood two deep. On the dance floor, couples were trying to dance, but couldn't hear the piano. Most of the men didn't know how to dance anyway, and could only stamp their feet. "Hey, barkeep." The drunken voice rose above the noise. "Fill 'er up again. It's by God payday."

Shoo, Todd said under his breath. This is no place to ask questions of anybody. He sidestepped, twisted and turned, and made his way to the bar. Not much chance of getting a bartender's attention.

Another drunken voice cut through the noise. "Hey you, you with the sorrel top, how 'bout a dance?"

Sorrel top? Todd looked around and saw her. Both of them. They had meant it when they said they were coming here. Leslie Manahan was standing at the far end of the bar, facing it. Her sister had her back to the bar, facing the crowd. Two half-filled shot glasses were on the bar near them. A drunk in miner's baggy pants and lace-up shoes was talking to Marietta Manahan. At her. She shrugged and turned her back to him.

Oh well, nobody is going to attack two women in a crowded place like this, Todd thought. They're safe enough. But he'd bet Leslie Manahan would sure like to get out of here.

He grinned when he thought about it. She wanted to leave, but she didn't want her sister to know it. She was staying to show her sister she wasn't afraid. That's how it looked to Todd. He shook his head, grinning. But in a way he felt sorry for her. She had to be mighty uncomfortable. Maybe he could help. He thought it over a moment, then began snaking his way to their end of the bar.

What he had in mind was to stand next to her, give

her somebody to talk to, somebody she could feel comfortable with, and let her wild sister do as she pleased. Yeah, she would appreciate that.

But another man got there first, got her attention, got nearly everyone's attention. It was the big, wide-shouldered, pug-faced man with the billy club and the Colt six-shooter.

Todd didn't get there in time to hear the first words he said, but he did hear Marietta Manahan answer, "Tell him if he wants to see me to come down here."

Pug Face growled, "He won't like that."

"Who gives a damn what he likes?"

"Come on." Pug Face took her by the arm and pulled. She pulled back.

"No."

"You're comin'."

"Leave her alone." It was Leslie Manahan, her voice high, thin, scared. "Take your hands off her."

"Shut up. She's comin'."

"Leave her alone." Now she was close to screaming.

Pug Face pulled, and Marietta Manahan's lace-up shoes slid in the sawdust. The Gold Palace was suddenly quiet.

"Whoa." Todd had reached the redhead's side. "Hold on. Just a damn minute, now."

Pug Face only glanced at Todd as he continued pulling on Marietta Manahan's arm. Her shoes dug furrows in the sawdust.

Leslie Manahan begged, "Let her go."

"I said, stop." Todd got his left hand on Pug Face's right shoulder and shoved hard. Pug Face let go his hold on the girl's arm and took a long look at Todd.

For a moment they faced each other. Todd knew the saloon bouncer was a killer. And that Colt six-

106

gun was carried low too, ready for a fast draw. Both men had their right hands close to their gun butts, fingers twitching.

Quiet. No one moved. No one spoke. A man was about to be killed. Some cowboy who dared challenge a saloon bouncer was about to be shot down.

Pug Face looked squarely into Todd's eyes. He saw no fear. His eyes moved down to the Remington. It was a gunfighter's weapon. This one wouldn't be easy.

Todd knew what was going on in the bouncer's mind. He was being paid to keep the peace and to carry out his boss's orders. If he had to kill to do his job he'd kill. He couldn't back down. Not from anyone.

Quiet.

Someone had to move first. Todd watched the bouncer's eyes, hoping they would signal his move. No one moved. No one spoke.

Except Leslie Manahan.

"Now . . . now wait a minute, gentlemen. You don't have to do this."

Her sister joined in, "Don't shoot. Either one of you. I'll . . . I'll go see Mister Hays." She moved carefully, but she got between the two men.

Todd spoke next, without taking his eyes off the bouncer's eyes, "You don't have to, Miss Manahan."

"I will. I'm not afraid of him." She moved around behind the bouncer and headed for the stairs. "Come on, Dog Face, your master wants you." The seat of her baggy overalls waggled as she walked.

Slowly, the bouncer turned, keeping his right hand close to the Colt and his eyes on Todd until his head had to follow his shoulders. When his back was to Todd, he walked with quick steps to the stairs.

"Oh my God." There was anguish in Leslie

107

Manahan's voice. "My God, my god. We almost caused someone to be killed." Her gray eyes were near tears as she turned them to Todd. "What's she doing up there? Who is Mister Hays?"

Todd had to let some of the tension drain out of him before he could answer, "I think he owns this place." His knees were suddenly weak and he had to order his hands not to tremble.

"You better be careful, mister," a miner said. "Nobody's stood up to old Hank before, and he ain't about to let you get away with it."

Leslie Manahan still was on the verge of tears. "What do you think they're doing up there?"

"I don't know," Todd answered. "But I'm staying here until she comes down. And if she doesn't come down pretty soon, I'm going up there."

CHAPTER TWELVE

He had everyone's attention, including the bartenders'. He ordered a beer. Miss Manahan declined another drink. Todd drank his beer in short swallows, keeping an eye on the stairs. The near-fight was soon forgotten by the crowd, and the racket returned. Shouting, laughing, cursing. The piano player pounded out a war tune, and a sawmill worker with sawdust on his hat brim led one of the saloon women to the dance floor.

Todd stared into his beer mug. What was he doing here, he asked himself. Good God, he'd almost killed a man or gotten killed because some crazy red-haired girl wanted to show her sister how brave she was. How dumb can you get, Todd Kildow? You've got better things to do than to die in some Colorado saloon over a girl who probably wouldn't spit on you. You just ran off at the mouth, that's what you did, saying you were going up those stairs after her. That would really be dumb. She's so damn brave. Says she can do anything a man can do. Let her take care of herself.

He glanced at Leslie Manahan. Her face was frozen as she watched the stairs. She was one damned scared young woman.

Give it a couple more minutes and he was going up

those stairs.

He ordered another beer, drank it. It was time.

Then he saw her coming.

She had her head up and a half-smile on her face as she came down the stairs. Pug Face, Dog Face, Hank, or whatever his name was came down two steps behind her. He stopped at the foot of the stairs and stood there, frowning at the crowd.

The crowd quieted and parted to make way for her as she walked back to the bar.

Leslie Manahan gasped, "What happened?"

"Nothing. Let's have another shot of booze."

"What do you mean, nothing? Something happened."

"Oh, he just wanted to talk to me, that's all. To make me another offer."

The noise was back, and Todd had to strain his ears to hear what was said.

"Another offer? What do you mean? Tell me, Marrie."

"All right. Do you want another drink?"

"No. Absolutely not. And neither do you."

"Just for that I'm going to have one." Marietta Manahan signaled a bartender and got her shot glass refilled. The bartender refused the money.

Miss Manahan shrugged with resignation. "I'm sorry, Marrie, I should have known better than to tell you what to do. Now will you tell me what's going on?"

"I used to work here."

"What?"

"Only for two days. Nights, I mean." When her sister sputtered something, Marietta Manahan went on, "It's not what you're thinking. I didn't go to bed with anyone. I just wanted to see what it was like. All

110

I did was dance with a few lonely miners and drink colored water. No harm done."

"Then what did this Mister Hays want?"

"He wants me to come back. Offered to double my pay. Only trouble is, he wants me to be his woman."

Todd almost choked over that. Some unlucky jasper might be this girl's man, but she wasn't going to be any man's woman.

"You refused, of course."

"Well, yeah, I refused. There. Does that make you feel better, sister dear?"

"Yeah," her sister said out of the side of her mouth. "Now let's get out of here."

The redhead picked up the shot glass, sniffed of it, put it down. "I don't like this damn stuff anyway. Here." She shoved the glass toward Todd. "You drink it." She turned to go, then added, "And don't be such a damn fool as to get killed over a barroom woman."

Damn fool is right. Todd sighed after they had gone. What did he come in here for anyway? Oh yeah, a woman named Lilly. Not much chance of finding her tonight. Maybe tomorrow when the place isn't so crowded. Yeah, tomorrow.

Hank, or whatever his name was, stood in his usual spot at the foot of the stairs. When Todd glanced his way their eyes met, but Todd looked away. The girl he was damn fool enough to fight over was gone. There was nothing to fight over now. Todd drank another mug of beer and worked through the crowd to the door.

The clerk at the Ponderosa Hotel had to be spending his nights as well as his days in a chair

111

behind the desk. He popped up out of the chair as soon as the door opened. "You're checking out in the morning?"

"No," Todd said, "I'm staying another day."

"You said you were leaving in the morning."

"I changed my mind. Ever change your mind?"

"Don't get smart, as we don't allow no smart alecks in here."

As soon as Todd made sure the door was locked and got his clothes off he plopped down on the feather bed and let out a long sigh. The things that had happened since he'd met Leslie Manahan. He was lucky to be alive.

Yeah, lucky.

That's what that stump-headed sheriff had said back in western Kansas. "As soon as the judge gets here and I can round up a jury, folks in Prairie County are gonna see how law and order works," Sheriff R.M. Hocker had said. "You'll be lucky if you don't hang."

Yeah, lucky that one of the Greener brothers was locked up in the same jail. The Greeners didn't stand for that. Too bad they killed a deputy. That deputy wasn't a bad feller. Lucky, though, that the Greeners unlocked all the cells while they were at it. Lucky that the sheriff concentrated on going after the Greeners, which gave Todd Kildow time to walk home, catch his best horse, pack some grub and light out.

That ten-mile trek home was something. After serving in the Union Army he was used to walking, but he wasn't used to looking over his shoulder, expecting to see the sheriff riding hard after him. Lucky.

But if he was so lucky, why did the whole thing have to happen in the first place? That was luck too.

Rotten luck.

Todd Kildow, also known as Douglas Brock, pulled a blanket up over his naked body, turned over on his side and went to sleep.

His horses were well fed and contented when he checked on them next morning. He recognized Marietta Manahan's dun horse in the next pen. He was well fed too.

When he saw the Manahan sisters in the working man's café, he was a little bit surprised, but when he thought about it he shouldn't have been. Leslie Manahan had already shown she wasn't the snooty, uppity type, and her sister would look out of place anywhere but in a working man's café.

The older sister waved him over to their table. She was wearing her long dress again. The younger one still had on her baggy overalls. "Good morning, Doug. Have some breakfast on us. The Manahan girls are in your debt."

The red-haired one said nothing.

"Naw, you don't owe me anything. But I could use some breakfast." He pulled out a chair and sat.

"I asked you before, Doug, and I know it's none of my business, but would you mind if I ask again what your plans are?"

"Oh . . ." He didn't know what to say. "I'm gonna stay around here another day or two."

"Then what?"

"Then what?" He wished he hadn't sat at their table. "I don't know."

"I'll make you an offer. Come back to Texas with me. I can guarantee you a job with the Quarter Circle C and top wages, good chuck and a real bed to sleep in."

113

He glanced at the younger sister. She was looking at him with that half-smile again. "Well, that's a good offer, Miss Manahan, and I appreciate it, but . . ."

The younger one spoke. "You like being foot-loose and fancy free, don't you?" She still wore that amused look.

"Yeah." Todd stared back at her. "As a matter of fact I do."

The half-smile slipped, then was back.

"I'm not offering you a job merely out of gratitude, Doug. The Quarter Circle C can always use a good honest dependable man. You would have a future there."

"You're looking for something, aren't you?" The younger sister was stating a fact.

He was grateful for the waitress, who interrupted before he had to answer. The café was out of eggs, but there was plenty of bacon, pancake batter and coffee.

They ate silently, the way cowboys did. The Manahan sisters were ranch girls, all right. It was obvious they didn't mind taking their meals with the hired help. Not until they had cleaned their platters and were sipping their coffee did anyone speak again.

"I have to go back," Leslie Manahan said. "I'm taking the stage to Denver this morning. I'll wire dad that Marrie is alive and well. I wish I could say she's safe."

A small giggle came from the other one. "After what happened the last time you got on a stage, I reckon I'm safer here."

Todd was trying to think of a way to say goodbye when they were interrupted again. This time it was a tall, thin man with a silver star pinned on his dark finger-length coat. Todd recognized him as the lawman he'd seen in the street a couple of nights ago.

"Oh, Miss Manahan." He took off his hat and stood at their table. "I heard you found your sister. I'm real happy about that."

"Won't you sit down, Mr. Garrick."

The lawman had brown hair streaked with gray and a carefully trimmed moustache. Without hesitating a second, he pulled out a chair and sat. "I had no idea, however, that your sister was the young woman I knew as Sorrel Top."

"You knew her, then?"

"Wa'al, not very well. I'd seen her in the Gold Palace, that's all. I heard somebody call her Sorrel Top."

The redhead spoke. "You never would have guessed that I'm related to a proper lady like Les."

The lawman was embarrassed. Todd read the inscription on his badge. He was a deputy U.S. Marshal, not a sheriff. Colorado didn't have county sheriffs. Todd wanted nothing to do with any lawman, especially a U.S. lawman.

"Wa-al no, I, I might have got wise sooner or later, but I've been pretty busy lately, what with that Indian prowling around, scaring the stuffing out of folks."

"Indian?" Marietta Manahan's eyebrows went up. "I thought the Utes were friendly."

"Most of them are, but this one is real strange. He's been seen prowling around at night, looking in windows, always by himself. Two men took a shot at him night before last, but they don't think they hit him. He disappears in the dark. We looked for him yesterday, but an army of Indians could hide in those woods."

"Looking in windows?"

"Yes, ma'am. He hasn't hurt anybody yet, but he's

got some folks scared."

For the third time, they were interrupted. This time it was the shotgun messenger Todd had seen on the stage. He stepped inside, looked around, spotted Leslie Manahan, and announced, "Stage's leavin' in a minute, Miss Manahan." He ducked out.

Standing, she opened her pocketbook, took out several bills and dropped them on the table. "This will pay for everyone. It's time for me to go."

Todd started to object to her paying for everyone, but she was halfway to the door. Her sister followed, and he followed her sister. The lawman stayed where he was.

Not knowing whether to say goodbye, Todd kept his distance until they reached the Palace Hotel where the stage was waiting. Six horses were stamping their feet nervously and snorting. There, Leslie Manahan motioned him over and put out her hand to shake.

"Thank you very much, Doug. My offer will always be good. Come anytime. I'll be happy to see you."

"It was my pleasure, Miss Manahan, and good luck." He shook with her briefly and turned away.

It was none of his business and he knew he shouldn't do it, but he had to look back. The two girls hugged each other. The older one was too emotional to speak, and the younger one said, "Tell Dad that I'll ... I'll come home one day. One day you'll all look up and I'll be there."

That was too much for Todd. Too personal. He left. But he did hear Miss Manahan say one more thing before she got into the stage.

"God be with you, Marrie."

*　　*　　*

He sat on a wooden bench at the livery barn with his head down and remembered his mother saying the same thing when he went away to war. They were God-fearing folks, his mother and dad. When they farmed in eastern Kansas they went to church every Sunday morning. Todd too. And his dad always gave thanks before every meal. Todd grew up that way. Not until they moved out West where churches were few and far between did they quit spending their Sunday mornings worshiping the Almighty.

He raised his head when Marietta Manahan walked by. She passed within thirty feet of him on her way to the corrals behind the barn. She nodded at him but didn't speak. He nodded back. In a few minutes she rode away on her dun horse, the Winchester rifle in a boot under her right knee.

Watching her ride down Main Street, Todd shook his head sadly, wondering whether he would ever see the Manahan sisters again. Weren't they something? And he wondered too about the prowling lone Indian the lawman had talked about. He knew that Indian.

What the purple hell was that blanket-ass up to?

CHAPTER THIRTEEN

The bartender at the Gold Palace had time on his hands again. "Yeh, there's a woman named Lilly works here, but she ain't here this time of day." He leaned over the bar and put his elbows on it. "I seen what happened last night. If you keep comin' in here you and old Hank're gonna have a shootout. He's dangerous."

"Yeah." Todd took another swallow of beer. "I'd stay clear of him but I've got to talk to this Lilly."

"Whatta you have to talk to her about?"

"Ever hear of a man named Hooter Wilson?"

"He's one of the two got killed tryin' to rob the bank."

"You didn't happen to know him, did you?"

"Seen 'im round, is all. Lilly knew 'im. Is that why you want to see her?"

"He might be the man I was looking for. I'd like to find out for sure."

"Oh, yeh, you said you was lookin' for some jasper from Kansas. Ever'body is from somewhere else. Me, I'm from Nebraska, and old Hank is from down south somewhere, and J.D., I heard he's from Saint Louie."

"J.D.?"

"Hays. J.D. Hays. The gent that owns this place."

"Oh, him."

The bartender had to go draw a beer for another customer, but before he left he said, "Come back tonight and Lilly'll be here, but don't start no ruckus. Old Hank'll be lookin' for a chance to peel your knob with that billy club or put a bullet in you."

"A ruckus," Todd muttered to the beer mug, "is the last thing I want."

Now it was Todd Kildow who had time to spare. No use knocking on that woman's door, wherever she lived. She probably stayed in the Gold Palace all night and slept all day, and wouldn't appreciate anybody knocking on her door.

He walked the length of the plank walk, crossed the street and walked down the other side. When he found himself at the livery barn, he decided to get on his horse and ride around the outskirts of town, see what there was to see. That decided, he saddled the young bay, paused. It would soon be dinnertime. Better to eat first. He didn't want to miss any meals. There was the mercantile. Some fresh bread would be good. With apple butter. Sure.

The bay snorted at the traffic on Main Street but was easy to handle. Todd could only hope he would stand tied at a hitchrack while he went into the store. A lean gent with a handlebar moustache and white apron around his middle sold him a loaf of fresh bread and a jar of apple butter, and Todd rolled it up in a rain slicker and tied it behind his saddle. Mounted again, he rode at a trot down Main Street to the northern edge of town. He crossed the river with little trouble from the bay, quit the road there and rode into the timber, following a dim trail.

He'd changed his mind. He didn't want to see the mines and sawmills. Instead he wanted to get out of town where it was quiet and the air was clean. Too much noise could have a man's head ringing so he couldn't think straight.

The tall ponderosas, lodgepole pines and spruce opened up into a wide meadow about three miles from the river where Todd reined up and dismounted. He picketed the horse with his catch rope, then unrolled the slicker and used his pocket knife to cut off a hunk of bread. It was good. Nothing better than fresh bread and apple butter. He ate half of it, sighed with contentment and lay back on the slicker with his hands under his head. The bay was having a good meal too on that mountain grass.

So much better than town. Quiet. Peaceful. He was the only human for many miles. He sighed again. Funny-looking squirrel. Black with long ears. Looking down on him from the limb of a ponderosa, wondering what kind of creature he was. It jerked its tail, chirped and ran up higher in the tree.

Suddenly Todd realized he wasn't the only human around.

He didn't know what warned him. The squirrel? A sixth sense? But he snapped to a sitting position with the Remington in his hand.

At first, when he saw him, he couldn't speak. Then he gulped and said, "What the hairy hell are you doing here?"

The Indian said nothing. Just sat on his heels twenty feet away. The long-bladed knife was in its fancy sheath hanging from his belt. Now, instead of a leather vest, he had on a white man's muslin shirt with the vest over it. Stolen, no doubt.

"What are you doing here?" Still no movement. "You'd better be careful, sneaking around town in the dark. Somebody took a shot at you once and the next time they won't miss. What the red-assed hell are you doing, anyway?"

121

The black eyes didn't blink, only stared at him.

Todd tried to remember what little he'd learned about Indian sign language. Zeke had taught him some of the signs used by the plains Indians, but he wasn't sure he knew how to ask a question. Zeke would have known. He'd spent a good many years in the Indian Nation before drifting up to Kansas and working for Mr. Kildow. Todd was fascinated at the way Zeke could communicate with the Indians without speaking a word. Todd had learned something about the language before Zeke drifted on. But how to ask a question? Well, he'd try.

Holding his left hand shoulder high, palm out, he waggled his hand back and forth, right then left. It worked. Or did it?

Still squatting on his heels, the red man made a V of two fingers on his right hand and held them horizontally under his right eye, pointing out in front.

"Hunting, huh? Hunting what? With what? That toad-stabber?"

No answer.

"Are you hungry? Here." Todd held out half-loaf of bread. "Come and get it, but keep your hands off that Arkansaw toothpick."

The Indian stared at him a moment, then stood. Todd kept the Remington handy. "Come ahead, but be damned careful. This gun can fire by itself."

With slow but determined steps, the red man walked closer and held out his hand. Todd handed him the bread. The Indian took it, turned his back to Todd and started to leave.

"Here. You might as well have this too." Todd held out the half-filled jar of apple butter. The Indian came back, took it, and walked away with rapid steps. He disappeared in the woods.

Shoo, Todd muttered. That savage has got a way of sneaking up on a man. He could have cut my throat. I ain't taking any more naps around here. He stood, rolled up his slicker and went to his horse.

The crowd wasn't as thick tonight in the Gold Palace. Todd reckoned the miners had already spent their pay, or what they could afford to blow in a saloon. The ricky-tick piano could be heard now. Pug Face stood in his usual spot at the foot of the stairs and wore the usual scowl. His eyes bored into Todd, daring him to start something. Todd ignored him and motioned to the bartender.

"Yeh, she's here," the bartender said, pointing. "Right over there. Just a minute, I'll send her over."

Todd watched him move down the bar to a young woman with long brown hair. She too wore a dress that was skimpy in the right places. After a long look at Todd, she came toward him, swinging her hips.

Not bad, but couldn't trot in harness with Leslie Manahan.

"You wanta see me?"

"Is your name Lilly?"

"Yeh, what's yours?"

"Douglas Brock. I've been told you were well acquainted with a gentleman named Hooter Wilson."

"Buy me a drink?"

"Sure."

He had an urge to snatch the glass away before she could drink its contents, just to see what would happen, but naw, this wasn't the time for that.

"Who're you lookin' for?"

"I believe his name was Hooter Wilson."

She threw her head back and laughed. Cackled,

rather. "If you're a lawdog you're too late. He's dead."

"I'm not a lawdog. I came to White River looking for a man, and he could have been the man."

"Why was you lookin' for him?"

"Tell me something, did he ever brag about escaping an ambush in western Kansas? Two men were killed there and one got away. It could have been him."

"I'm powerful thirsty."

The bartender was right there. Todd paid.

"Hooter was always braggin' about his gunfights and his robberies and stuff, but I don't recollect him sayin' anything about an ambush in Kansas."

"I was told he came from Kansas."

"Yeh. That's what he said. Kansas City."

"And I was told he came here about a year ago."

A frown of concentration appeared on her face, and she answered, "Almost a year ago. He came up here from Denver."

"Then he could have come through western Kansas on his way to Denver, before he came up here?"

"Yeh. Could of. Prob'ly did."

"But he didn't say anything about robbing anybody in western Kansas or escaping from an ambush?"

"Not that I recollect."

"Damn." Todd was silent a moment, then, "Did he have any other friends? I mean, who did he hang around with?"

"He had all kinds of friends. He had a way of making everybody think he was the best fella in the world. You'd trust him with anything. He was that kinda man."

Lilly's mouth tightened then, and a hard glint came into her eyes. "He'd cut your throat for a dollar."

124

"I believe I've met one or two like that."

"He had another woman, too. A whore. She works over at the Buckhorn."

"Yeah, I know. Where did he hang around most?"

"There or here. He spent a lot of time in here. Gambling."

"Is there anybody he was specially friendly with?"

"Naw. I seen him talkin' to Hank over there sometimes, and I seen him talkin' with Mister Hays sometimes, and, like I said, he was a talker, Hooter was, but when it was bedtime he had to have a woman."

"Why would he be talking with Mister Hays? I mean, why would he be talking with a successful businessman?"

She shrugged. "I dunno. Like I said, he was a con man, a bunko steerer. Only he talked too goddamn much. That mouth of his might of got him killed."

"Yeah? How's that?"

"He told me he was gonna rob the bank, but he didn't have a chance. Him and his sidekick. They were shot so full of holes so fast they didn't even have a chance to give up."

"You think maybe somebody blew on them? Warned the bank?"

"I dunno. Could be. I dunno."

"Who could have done it?"

Another concentration wrinkle. She opened her mouth to speak, then closed it. Finally, she reached a decision and said, "Beats the hell out of me. Time for another drink!"

This was running into money and nowhere else. He laid a half-dollar on the bar and tried to think of more questions. He said, "Thanks. Have another one on me."

Another deadend. Another blind canyon. Too many blind canyons. He walked to the livery barn, found it locked and went out to the corrals. There, he leaned on a fence, recognized his horses in spite of the dark, and watched them doze lazily. Like to get out of there, wouldn't you? Don't blame you. Keeping a horse in a pen is like keeping a man in jail. Well, we'll be on our way pretty soon, probably tomorrow. No use hanging around here. Damned if I know where we'll go. Maybe back to Texas. Miss Manahan offered me a job. That's probably a good place to go. Yeah, we'll head out first thing in the morning.

But he didn't. When he went to the corrals to feed his horses next morning the pack horse was lame.

"Uh-oh." Quickly, he crawled between the corral poles. "What's the matter, old feller? It's the left fore, ain't it?" He ran his hands down the left front leg, picked up the foot, examined the bottom of it, and went looking for the hostler.

"I'm real sorry, mister. Somebody opened the gate by accident, and your horse got in a pen with some other horses. He got kicked. Ain't nothin' broke, but I think he's got a bruised left shoulder. He'll be all right in a day or so."

Jaws clamped tight, Todd went back to the horse and rubbed the left shoulder. No reaction from the horse. He rubbed the shoulder again, hard. The horse stepped away from him. The hostler stayed outside the pen and watched.

"That's what it is," Todd said, "a bruise. He can move around good enough to feed, but he can't go very far."

"I'm real sorry, mister. I ain't responsible for anything, you know, but I'm real sorry. Was you plannin' on usin' him?"

"Yeah. I'll wait a day or two and if he's still lame

I'll have to sell him or trade him off."

Back in his room at the Ponderosa Hotel, he lay on the bed a while, sat up, lay down, walked the floor, looked out the window, and put his hat on and went down on the street. With nothing else to do, he went to the Gold Palace, thinking he'd at least find somebody to talk to. Now he knew why cowboys got into trouble when they hung around town too long. Hell, there was nothing else to do.

The bartender with the waxed moustache—Bob, he'd heard somebody call him—drew a beer and set it before him. "Learn anything from Lilly?"

"Naw. Only that Hooter Wilson was a talker. But I reckon he didn't say anything I care to know about."

"He was a talker, all right."

"Way I understand it, he might have shot his mouth to the wrong feller and the bank got wind of his plan to rob it."

"They was ready for him, all right, but they're always ready over there."

"You don't think anybody warned the bank, then?"

"Could be." Bob thought it over. "Yeah, could be. Come to think of it, they was waiting for him and his pal to come out, then filled 'em full of lead before they got two steps farther."

"Or maybe somebody got suspicious when they saw that pair go into the bank."

"That could be too. But the way I heard it, nobody told them to throw up their hands or anything, just popped away. Their carcasses were so full of holes the doc couldn't count 'em all."

"Kind of odd," Todd mused aloud.

"Yeah, but I'll tell you one thing, nobody's tried to rob the bank since then."

"No." Todd grinned, shaking his head. "That

127

could sure discourage a feller."

One beer was enough. Somehow it didn't taste as good in the morning, and he didn't feel like drinking whiskey either. The street was full of wagons, buggies and horsebackers. He stood on the plank walk, leaning a shoulder against one of the pine posts that held up the roof over the walk. Two freight wagons went by, loaded so heavily with ore from a mine that it took six horses to pull each one. A lumber wagon passed. Two men on horseback. A little man in a floppy hat and overalls approached on a dun horse.

A little man? Hell, that was Marietta Manahan. She was riding at a slow walk, and she had two gunny sacks half-full of something hanging from the front of her saddle, one on each side of the horse. Rocks? Yeah, looked like it.

Without moving, he watched her rein up across the street in front of a door that had a sign above it. The sign read: ASSAYER. When she started to lift one of the sacks down from the saddle, he ambled over to help.

"Morning, Miss Manahan. Let me give you a hand here."

"Oh. Doug. You still in town?" Her face was bright and cheerful. "Guess what?"

Her happy smile rubbed off on him, and he grinned too. "I can't begin to guess."

"This," she said, lifting one of the sacks, "is very rich gold ore."

"You're joshing."

"Nope. You, Douglas Brock, are looking at a very rich woman."

His grin widened. "No."

"Yep. I just struck it rich."

128

CHAPTER FOURTEEN

He helped her carry the sacks inside the assayer's office and set them on a big scarred desk. The assayer, a young man wearing a green eyeshade, was working in the back of the room with something smoking and bubbling.

"Just leave them there," he said. "It'll be a while."

"Hurry, will you?"

"It'll be a while."

With a shrug, she went to the door. Todd followed. Outside, she untied her horse from the hitchrail, then re-tied him. "This is the time for a celebration." She looked at Todd. "A woman doesn't like to celebrate alone, and I don't have many friends in White River. How about a shot of whiskey?"

"Thought you didn't like the stuff."

"Only on special occasions. This, my brave male friend, is a special occasion."

"You're not gonna start any fights, are you?"

She shot him a frown. "If I do, I'll finish it. You stay out of it."

"Agreed."

Bob, the bartender, recognized her immediately. "Hey, Sorrel Top, what fetched you back to this den of sin?"

"Pour us some whiskey, Bob. Good whiskey. And

wipe that silly grin off your face. You just might be looking at the next owner of this establishment."

"You goin' into the saloon business, are you, Sorrel Top?"

"Who knows. I can go into any business I want to. I just struck the mother lode. I'm rich."

"The hell you say." Surprise spread across Bob's face.

"Yup. Pour one for yourself. I'm buying."

Bob hurried down the bar to find three clean shot glasses, and he reached under the bar for a bottle of whiskey.

"What are you gonna do, Sorrel—Miss Manahan?" Todd asked. "Mine it yourself or sell your claim?"

"Now that's gonna take some thinking." She picked up her whiskey, tossed it down her throat, and nearly strangled. "Ga-a-w-ud." Tears ran down her face.

Chuckling, Todd merely shook his head and sipped his whiskey. "Let me buy you another."

She gasped, "In a minute. Wait till that one stops smoking."

"That's the best whiskey in the house, Sorrel Top. Or should I call you Lady Manahan now?"

Still breathless, she said, "I knew there was a reason I don't like whiskey. Whoo. Don't light any matches around me, I'll blow up."

Todd chuckled. He wanted to say something like it takes a man to drink whiskey and maybe she wasn't so damned masculine after all, but he thought better of it.

"What are you gonna do with your find, Sorrel Top?"

"I don't know. Depends on how much I'm offered for it. If I mine it myself, I'll have to build a road to it

130

and buy some mining machinery. I don't know." She smiled, and Todd noticed that she had some of her sister's good looks. "But I'm gonna have a lot of fun deciding."

"Don't let 'em buy it too cheap, Sorrel Top. There's men gettin' rich around here buyin' up claims that these old sourdoughs ain't got the money to mine."

"Don't worry about Yours Truly. If I need the money, I can get it." She paused, then said, "I reckon I'll go across the street and hear the good news. You gents keep your powder dry." She left, the seat of her baggy overalls flopping and wagging.

Todd wanted to go with her, but he wasn't asked. After she left he went out and leaned against the roof support again. He grinned to himself. Some girl. Left a wealthy home and went out on her own just to show the world—and maybe herself—she could do it. And now she's struck it rich. He shook his head, grinning.

But when he saw her come out of the assayer's office he knew something was wrong.

Her face was blank. She moved stiffly, like a wooden woman. With clumsy fingers, she untied her dun horse and started to mount. Todd went over.

"What happened, Miss Manahan?"

She gave him a blank look, and spoke in a low monotone. "Pyrite. I should have known. Fools gold. I'm a fool."

He wanted to say something sympathetic as she climbed on her horse, turned him around and rode away. He didn't know what to say. She rode down Main Street at a slow trot and turned toward the river, sitting slumped in the saddle.

Shaking his head sadly now, Todd walked back to the livery pens to take another look at his lame horse.

131

Too bad, he mused. Must be a hell of a blow, thinking you're rich and finding out you're not. The horse hadn't improved. It would be a couple of days before he could travel.

Disappointed and disgusted, he went back to his hotel, thinking about his own problems, and about Marietta Manahan. He wondered what would become of her. He wondered if he would ever see her again.

He did. That same night.

It took a while for the noise to work through to Todd's brain, and when it did he sat up with a snort. "Huh? What?"

The knocking persisted.

"What?" He got out of bed and pulled on his pants, then his boots. "What?" he yelled through the hotel room door. "Who's there?"

"It's Mister Slaughter," a man's voice said through the door.

Slaughter? Who the square-headed hell is Mister Slaughter? Oh. The owner. "What do you want?"

"There's a woman downstairs to see you. She wouldn't wait til morning."

"A woman?"

"Yah. She looks more like a man."

Marietta Manahan? "I'll be right down." He buttoned his shirt and stuffed the tail of it in his pants. The Remington in its holster went on next. Then his hat. He clumped down the stairs, sounding like a herd of buffalo, and stopped when he saw her standing by the desk. Her face was white and pinched.

"Doug," she said in a wavering voice, "I need to talk to you." She swallowed hard and forced her voice down. "I apologize for waking you up, but I need to talk to you."

"We don't allow no women in the men's rooms."

He shot a mean look at Mister Slaughter. "Sure, Miss Manahan. Let's go outside."

She headed for the door with him behind her. The night air was cold. He shivered, wishing he'd worn his duck jacket. She didn't have a jacket on either, just a cotton shirt and the overalls. Heavy shoes and the floppy hat. A few of the town's windows were lighted. The Gold Palace still had its outside lamps lighted, but in most directions the town was dark.

"What happened?" They stood on the plank walk just outside the hotel door.

She stuttered, stopped, stuttered again, and finally got out, "Two men were killed. At my cabin. I . . . don't know what happened."

"Oh boy," Todd groaned. "Two men killed. Did you go to the law?"

"Yes. I mean I tried to. He's out of town. In Denver. I'm sorry to bother you, but I don't know anyone else I can trust."

"How?"

"I wish there were some place we could talk. I mean, sit down and talk, but I don't know of any place."

"Let's go over to the livery corrals. Where's your horse?"

"Right here. I'll get him."

Leading her horse, she walked beside Todd to the livery barn and behind it. They sat on the ground in the dark. She hugged her knees. Todd shivered.

"I don't know exactly what happened, Doug. It's so strange I can't believe it myself."

He could barely see her face. "Tell me what you saw."

133

"I didn't follow your advice, and left my rifle behind when I went to water my horse this evening. It was close to dark." She paused, then went on. "Two men, men I've never seen, were there. They grabbed me and carried me back to my cabin. I kicked and screamed, though I knew there wasn't anyone around to help. They almost had me to the cabin when . . ."

She had to stop again. Though he couldn't see her in the dark, he knew she was trying to control herself. He ordered himself to quit shivering, and remained silent.

"I . . . I really don't know exactly what happened. At first I thought it was an animal, a cougar or something. It just appeared and it was so quick and furious I didn't even get a good look at it. I think it was a man. It had to be a man because it had a long knife. It happened so fast and I was so scared, I really didn't even see what happened. It . . . those two men are dead. Stabbed."

"Shoo." It took him a moment to absorb it all, then, "What did you do?"

"I ran. At first I just ran. Then I regained my senses and went back and got my horse. The marshal isn't here. I . . . I'm afraid to go back by myself. Can I hire you, Doug, to go back with me?"

"Sure. You don't have to pay me. I've got time on my hands anyway. The only thing is . . ."

"What, Doug?"

He didn't know whether to say it. If he did, she would be suspicious. It would be a mistake to tell anyone. Especially a woman.

"You've got trouble yourself, haven't you Doug?"

"Naw. But I never did get along with lawmen. I just as soon not have anything to do with the marshal when he comes back."

She considered that. "I see. As far as I'm concerned you won't have to. In fact, I'll make sure you're left out of anything I tell the marshal."

"I'd appreciate it."

They were quiet a moment, then he asked, "You said the animal or whatever it was had a knife?"

"Yes. It had a knife and long hair. It was a man, but I only got a quick glimpse of him."

"Could he have been an Indian?"

"Yes, he could have. Come to think of it he probably was."

"I think I know him. I don't know what he's doing around here, though."

"Well, whatever he is, whoever he is, he saved my life."

"Yeah, that he did. I wonder why?"

It was a long time until daylight. He suggested she get a room at one of the hotels. He'd wake her up when daylight came. No, she was too tense to sleep. They'd have to wait for morning to get his saddle out of the livery barn, and they'd freeze to death before then. She said nothing, just shivered. All right, he'd go back to his room and get a jacket. With his jacket on she wasn't too uncomfortable, but he was still cold. He tried not to let her know it. At times he stood, waved his arms and stamped his feet to get the blood circulating.

While they waited he had time to think, and he knew he'd made a mistake. Picking up dead bodies was a job for lawmen. If the marshal wasn't around, then he must have appointed someone else to do whatever law work needed doing. Not only that, what was he going to do when he and the woman got back to her cabin?

Well, he'd just stand by while she gathered what belongings she needed and then come right back to

135

town. She could tell her story to whoever wanted to listen, and if someone took it on himself to do something with these bodies, he'd be in the clear.

Yeah, that's what he'd do. Stay in the clear.

How the sizzling hell did he get in this mess anyway?

Daylight was just a small glow on the eastern horizon. Gradually it grew until it spread to the town of White River. A burro brayed somewhere. Dogs barked. By then she was lying on her side with her knees drawn up and her hands between her knees, using her hat for a pillow. Strands of long sorrel hair covered her face, reminding him that she was a woman. It reminded him too—he grinned a wry grin when he thought about it—that she wasn't as tough as she thought she was. He wanted hot coffee so bad he almost couldn't stand it, but he didn't want to be seen in the café with her. She could go to the café herself if she wanted to. She didn't want to.

When the livery man showed up and unlocked the barn, she took her horse to the alley behind the mercantile and waited for him there. He lied to the livery man about not being able to sleep and deciding to get on his horse and go look around, try to find a likely spot to dig for gold. The livery man stared at him in disbelief, but minded his own business.

They got across the river without being noticed. He hoped.

Conversation was light as they rode side by side on the wagon road. When they left the road and went up the trail along a creek it was single-file traveling, and he took the lead. The willows they had to push through were wet with dew. When they came out they were wet themselves and blue with cold. Come on, sunshine.

Eventually, the sun came up over the eastern ridge, shining through the trees and warming them. When they rode out of the timber into the park where her cabin was, he was both relieved and worried. He'd seen his share of dead men in the war, but the sightless eyes of the dead always made him uncomfortable. He knew how liquid left the eyes after a time, leaving the eyes sunken and grotesque. At least, this time, he wouldn't have to move the bodies, just stand there while she packed her stuff. Unless one was blocking the door. He hoped not.

As they approached the cabin, he glanced at her and saw she was nervous and scared. Then when they were within fifty feet of the cabin door, she reined up sharply and sucked in her breath.

"What . . . where?"

There were no bodies.

CHAPTER FIFTEEN

Marietta Manahan gasped. "They were right there. Right by the door. I know they were."

Todd considered that, then said, "Well, they weren't dead. That's the only explanation."

"But they were. They were bleeding something awful and they weren't moving."

Half turning in his saddle, he faced her. "Ever seen a dead man, Miss Manahan?"

"Once. One of our cowboys was killed by the Comanches. I . . . didn't like looking at him."

"Well then, you didn't take a good look at those two. Dead men don't get up and leave."

She shook her head. "I can't believe it. I just can't believe it."

"Listen, Miss Manahan, what happpened to you would have scared me too when I was your age. Before the war. I probably would have done exactly what you done."

Her shoulders slumped and she dismounted and led her horse to the cabin door. She dropped the reins and looked as if she didn't know whether to open the door or not.

Still on horseback, Todd said, "There's blood. Somebody bled a lot. Somebody was hurt, that's for sure. I'll take a look around."

He reined the bay back to the creek, then started a big circle around the cabin. There were hoofprints. The two men had horses. That helped them get away after the girl had left. A deep hole gaped in front of him, and he rode close enough to look down into it. A prospector's hole. That was where she'd dug up the pyrite. It was a good seven feet deep, and it had been dug with a pick and shovel. Damned hard work. Especially for a woman. He rode another hundred yards and found another prospector's hole. This one was only three feet deep.

In the woods now, he studied the ground for more hoofprints, footprints, blood, anything.

He rode out of the woods and was at the back side of the cabin, fifty feet away from it, when he saw the grave.

The sight of it sent a shiver up his back. He had the feeling he was being watched, and he glanced around nervously. It was a grave, no doubt about that. The meadow grass had been turned over and the dirt was fresh. The right size for a man or two men, one on top of the other.

Miss Manahan was right. They were dead. Dead and buried.

Riding back, the shiver was running up and down his spine, and he wished he were somewhere else. She hadn't moved much, still standing where he'd left her. A shovel and pick were leaning against the side of the cabin. Someone had put them back where he'd found them. The dun horse was cropping the grass nearby. Her eyes searched his face.

"You saw something."

"Yeah. A grave. One or both of them are buried back there."

140

"Who could have done it?"

"The same man who killed them."

"Why? And why did he protect me?"

"Now that's a question I can't answer. I wish I could." He dismounted. "Have you been inside?"

"Not yet." She turned toward the door, hesitated a second, squared her shoulders and pushed the door open. Todd watched as she went in, came out. "There are some things on the table. I don't know what."

"Things?" He took another nervous look around and went inside. Piled on the table were two skinning knives, some money, both paper and silver, matches and nothing else. "Guns," Todd said. "They had to have had guns. He's armed now."

"Who is?"

"The Indian. The Cheyenne."

"Yes, you mentioned an Indian. What about him?"

Instead of answering, Todd said, "I don't see anything here that would identify those two."

She came over and took a closer look, shuddered. "I wonder who they were?"

"We might never know." He turned and went back outside. She followed. "What do you want to do, Miss Manahan? Stay here or go back to town?"

"I don't think I want to stay here. Would you?"

"If I was in your place, no. No reason to. If there's any gold around here, you won't find it. You haven't had the experience. Whose cabin is this, anyway?"

"Mine. I bought it."

"From who? A prospector?"

"No. From a trapper. He trapped beavers and weasels and things. He said the creek is empty of beaver now."

Todd looked over the cabin, from the tarpaper roof

to the heavy timbers used for a foundation. "Not a bad wickiup. A feller could lay in some chuck, do a little hunting, and live out the winter in there. But I don't know as I'd want to."

"I wasn't planning to spend the winter here. I've bought another cabin in White River. It's where I lived for a few months until I got this one."

A small smile swept across Todd's face and was gone. "You're a real land baron. If you don't want to stay here, let's pack your stuff and go back to town. Those bodies'll keep until the marshal gets back to dig them up. I'm glad I don't have to do it. You can tell him what happened. If I told him he wouldn't believe it." Chuckling, he added, "I wouldn't believe it myself if I hadn't . . ."

He didn't finish what he'd started to say. Instead his head swiveled around in the direction Miss Manahan was looking. Her mouth was open and she whispered: "It's him."

Todd's hand went to the Remington, but he didn't draw it. He stood still watching the Indian walk toward them out of the woods. Marietta Manahan remained perfectly still, mouth open.

The Indian was armed now. A six-gun in a holster was strapped around his waist, and another hung by its cartridge belt from his left shoulder. He carried a lever-action rifle over his right shoulder, butt forward to show he didn't intend to use it.

When he came closer, she gasped, "That's my Winchester. I forgot it."

"Don't move," Todd warned. "Maybe he's friendly."

The young savage was still dressed in his Indian britches and moccasins, white man's shirt and leather vest. His black hair hung down to his shoulders. Fifty feet from the two whites he stopped.

142

For a long moment no one moved. Then the Indian raised his left hand shoulder high with the index and middle fingers together. Slowly, he raised the hand until it was level with the top of his head. That done, he dropped his hand and stood motionless.

She whispered. "What is he doing?"

"I'm not sure, but I think he's harmless." Todd made the same motion with his left hand. He forced himself to smile, but he couldn't relax. Never trust an Indian, he'd been warned. Often.

But when the savage squatted on his heels and put his guns on the ground, relief spread over Todd. What more could a man do to show he meant no harm? Todd made the sign with his left hand again. The Indian stood and walked toward them.

"What should we do?" she whispered.

"Nothing now. Wait."

Twenty feet away, the red man squatted again, this time sitting cross-legged.

"Let's sit down too," Todd said. He sat cross-legged the same way. The woman followed suit.

Todd held his right hand out, palm up, and bent his wrist to the left and then to the right.

"What does that mean?"

"I hope it means I want to ask him a question. I want to ask him why he saved you and buried the bodies."

The Indian pointed first to Todd and then to the woman. Face blank now, he held his right hand flat against his heart and moved it out level with the heart.

Todd nodded his head to let the Indian know he understood. "I think he's saying we are good people."

Again the Indian raised his hand shoulder high

143

with the two longest fingers extended, and again he raised the hand higher. He pointed to Todd and then to the woman.

Todd considered that, and said, "I think he's saying I'm a friend and he saw us together and that makes you a friend. That would explain it. He saw what was happening to you and took it on himself to save you."

She faced him and smiled a weak smile. "I thank you. You saved my life. I'm in your debt."

Still no expression on the Indian's face. This time he put his hand under his chin and pointed up at it. Then he made a fist and brought it down fast, opening his fingers. Next he moved his fist back and forth, and let it drop. It was a sign Todd had seen before from the Indian.

"I get it. He said the men were bad and he made war on them."

"Boy, did he ever. They won't attack a woman again."

"Nope. He was prosecutor, judge, jury and executioner. That's the way it has to be . . ." Todd paused when he realized he was describing himself, making an excuse for himself . . . "sometimes."

"Right. There's no law around here. They would have gotten away with it and I would probably be dead. I do owe him a great deal. How did you two get to be friends?"

"It's a long story." He didn't want to tell the story, and as it turned out he didn't have to. Before he could answer, the Indian stood, held his right hand up, palm out, turned and walked away.

After making the same sign, Todd stood and watched as the Indian picked up the two pistols, leaving the rifle, and walked on into the woods.

"Well," he said, finally, "that makes us even. I

144

saved his life, in a manner of speaking, and he saved yours. But I wonder what he's doing around here."

"He was watching me, that's for sure. And now that I think of it, another mystery had just been solved. I had a shank of cured ham in there and some of it was missing when I got back from White River. At first I thought I had eaten it and forgotten." She shuddered. "It gives me the shivers to think I was being watched, but I'm still alive because of it."

Todd went over to pick up the rifle. "This is a good gun. The best. If he was hunting, as I believe he said he was, he could sure use a gun like this." He studied the ground a moment, a frown pulling is eyebrows together. "Hunting. What the silly hell—excuse me, ma'am—what the heck is he hunting?"

He continued frowning at the ground, then said, "Well, let's get your stuff together and get back to town. You say you've got another cabin in town?"

"Yes. I bought it when I first came to White River. I won't have to take much."

While she packed clothes and a few cooking utensils in a carpetbag, he stood outside the door, looking in the direction the Indian had gone. "They had horses," he mused. "I saw the tracks. Now he's got horses. He can get around faster now. Wherever he wants to go he can go faster." Todd frowned at the ground again. "I'd give a dollar to know where it is he wants to go."

CHAPTER SIXTEEN

Marietta Manahan was more talkative when they rode back to town. Todd carried her carpetbag on the saddle in front of him. He didn't feel much like talking. All he wanted was to get out of this part of the country. He'd followed every lead he'd heard of and it was time to go.

"Where did you learn Indian sign language, Doug?"

"Huh? Oh, I learned it from a hired man on my dad's farm."

"Had you ever communicated with Indians before?"

"Oh, a little. Cheyennes."

"Cheyennes? Are there Cheyennes in Texas?"

Uh-oh. He'd slipped. "Uh, yeah, a few. I think all plains Indians use pretty much the same signs."

"Where does your father farm?"

This was getting dangerous. "Oh, uh, in west Texas."

"That takes in a lot of territory."

"Yeah, it does, doesn't it?" He hoped she'd get the message.

Looking down, her voice subdued, she said, "I'm sorry. It's none of my business. It's just that I'm curious, that's all."

"It's all right." He looked straight ahead.

Her cabin in town was the same as the one in the hills: one room, a tarpaper roof and a splintery wooden floor. It held a two-burner cookstove with a small oven, a sawed-wood table with aspen legs, two chairs, an iron cot, nails in the walls to hang cooking utensils and clothes on, and a large steamer trunk against a wall. A pole fence surrounded about an acre of land and a lean-to back of the cabin provided a windbreak and a roof for her dun horse. The cabin was three blocks from Main Street, with the river on the north. Todd would have bet it took a hell of a lot of stove wood to keep that cabin warm in the winter.

"This is home," she said when she opened the door and looked in. "It's not much, but it's shelter."

He carried her satchel inside, placed it on the table and turned to go. She opened it, took out a wallet and offered him some folding money.

"No. You don't need to pay me."

"But I promised to pay you."

"Naw."

"My sister asked you once, Doug, and got a vague answer. Do you mind if I ask again what your plans are?"

"I'll light out in another day or two. My pack horse is lame right now. When he's able to travel I'll head back south."

"Then you'll be here at least until tomorrow?"

"Looks like it."

"Good. Then I can cook you a meal. I'll hurry over to the mercantile and get some groceries. You'll let me do that much, won't you?"

"Well, I uh . . ."

That half-smile was back. "Think fast, Doug. What excuse are you going to use this time?"

He had to grin with her. "All right. When?"

148

"Tonight. Anytime after dark. Will you be here?"

"Sure, I'll be here."

Back at the livery pens, he fed his horses and pumped water for them. The pack horse was moving around better, but still not in shape for traveling. He hunted up the livery owner who was doing what he spent most of his time doing, shoveling manure. This time he was forking it from a pile beside the barn and throwing it into a wagon. The manure would fertilize someone's garden or nearby meadow.

"Do any horse trading?" Todd asked.

"Some."

"Got anything to trade for my lame horse?"

The man stuck his manure fork into the pile, put his hands on the small of his back and bent backward. "Uh," he grunted. "Get kinks in my back sometimes. Got a good brown horse that's half Percheron and he'll carry three hunnerd pounds without knowin' it. And he'll work in harness too."

"Where is he?"

"Ain't here right now. Lent 'im to a feller. Be back tomorrow."

"Well, if my horse is still lame tomorrow, I might try to trade with you."

"You'll have to pay some boot. That's a damn good horse, that brown is."

"How much more than my horse do you figure he's worth?"

"Fifty bucks."

"Unh-unh." Todd shook his head.

"Wait'll you see 'im."

"For fifty bucks I can wait 'til my horse gets well." He walked away shaking his head and muttering, "Some people, when they know your horse is lame and you want to travel, will cheat the hell out of you."

A beef sandwich in the café and back to the hotel. The clerk, manager, owner or whatever he was wore the same sour expression. "You ain't paid yet," he said as Todd started up the stairs.

"Oh yeah." Todd came back, reached for his roll of bills and paid. "I might have to stay tomorrow night too. Got a lame horse."

"You let us know in advance as we don't allow nobody to go sneakin' in their rooms without payin'."

"I knew you were gonna say that."

"And we don't allow no . . ."

Todd cut him off, "Yeah, I know, no smart alecks."

In his room, Todd rummaged through his warbag looking for some clean clothes. They were all soiled. Quickly, he gathered an armload, wrapped them in a shirt and hurried downstairs, out on the street, and into the laundry four doors down. Tomorrow, he was told. No sooner.

"Damn," he muttered on his way back to the hotel. "Should have taken some stuff over there when I first hit town." Back in his room, he poured the basin full of water, stripped off his shirt and washed it by hand, using a bar of yellow soap. Couldn't go to supper at a young woman's house in a dirty shirt. Not even a woman like Marietta Manahan. He wrung the shirt out and hung it in the open window, hoping the light breeze would dry it off, but knowing he was going to have to put it on wet. Hell, might as well wash everything else.

Downstairs, he pumped a bucket of water and carried it to his room. The clerk gave him a quizzical look, but kept his mouth shut for a change. Todd washed his undershorts and socks, but not his pants. They would have to do as is. He didn't want to hang his shorts in the window for everyone to see, so he wrung them and re-wrung them, then waved them in the air. He'd have to put them on wet too.

Now he was standing in his pants and nothing else. Good excuse for taking a nap, make up for some of the sleep he'd missed the night before.

It was dusk when he woke up.

His shorts and shirt were damp and clammy when he put them on. The shirt would dry soon after he went out in the breeze, but not the shorts. His socks were only a little damp, but damp enough that he had a hard time getting his boots on. Stamping his feet to get the socks settled in the right places, he went out to the livery pens where he fed and watered his horses. The pack horse was improving, but still favoring the left fore. He sat on the fence until after dark.

All right, he said to himself with resignation, like it or not he had to have supper with a lady. A woman, rather. Or what? Marietta Manahan, that's what. He could think of no way to describe her.

Surprise.

She answered his knock on the door immediately, and for a moment he thought he'd come to the wrong cabin. But no, that carrot-colored hair had to belong to the younger of the Manahan sisters.

"Come in, Doug." She smiled a real wide-open smile for the first time since he'd met her. A pretty smile. Good white teeth. But that wasn't the first thing he noticed.

She wore a dress. A long one. Down to her ankles and up to her neck, but pulled in at the waist. She wasn't as tall as her sister, but she had all the curves in the right places. Come to think of it, if she'd worked

151

at the Gold Palace, she had to have worn a dress there. One of those dresses that were low at the top and high at the bottom. She knew how to look like a woman. All he could do was stand outside the door and stare.

"Doug, are you going to stand there with a silly grin on your face or are you coming in?"

"I was expecting, uh . . ."

"You were expecting a woman who tries to act like a man. Pull up a chair and I'll pour you a cup of coffee."

He did and she did. He sipped the coffee. Something was cooking and it smelled good. She put on a white apron, slipping the top of it over her shoulder-length hair and tying the middle with a string. She opened the oven, looked in, shut the oven door and took a lid lifter from a nail on the wall. With a lid off the fire box, she shoved in another length of split firewood, then sat in a chair on the other side of the table from him.

His damp shorts were beginning to itch.

"I learned something about myself, Doug."

He didn't know what to say, so he waited for her to go on.

"I learned that I can't do everything a man can. I wouldn't have gone back to that cabin by myself for anything in the world. I needed a man."

Clearing his throat to get his voice working again, he said, "Well, I saw a couple of holes you dug looking for a vein, or whatever you prospectors look for, and it took a lot of hard, back-breaking work to dig those holes."

A wry smile touched her lips. "Yeah, I worked like a man. I worked like a fool. All I've got to show for it are a bunch of blisters." Self consciously, she glanced down at her hands. His eyes followed her glance, then moved back to her face and hair. Her hair had

152

been combed and brushed until it shone like polished copper, but her hands were rough and callused. The fingernails were broken.

"Miss Manahan, you asked me what my plans are. Can I ask you the same?"

She shrugged, looked down at her hands again. "Call me Marietta, or Marrie. I've been trying to figure out the answer to that question myself. I'm not going home. Not yet. And I don't care to go back to the Gold Palace."

"That's no work for a lady." Silently, he wondered if Leslie Manahan had told her sister about hiring him to look for her in the whorehouses. No, he reckoned, she didn't. And he sure as hell wasn't about to tell her.

Standing quickly, she took another look in the oven and shut the oven door. "Supper's ready. You'd never guess what it is. It's elk ribs. Roasted with potatoes. Ever eaten elk meat, Doug?"

"No. I've had deer and antelope, but not elk."

"You're in for a new experience then." She quickly added, "I didn't shoot it. I bought a few pounds of ribs from the man who did. He was selling it in the mercantile."

He watched as she used the bottom of her apron to take hold of an iron pot, lift it out of the oven and set it on top of the stove. When she opened the oven he saw a loaf of bread and two large potatoes inside. She took the lid off the pot, put it open-side up on one of the burners and used two forks to lift the meat out and onto the hot lid. Three heaping spoonsful of flour went into the pot and a half cup of water. She added more water a little at a time as she stirred.

"I think it's ready," she said finally, wiping a strand of red hair from her face. "I went right to the mercantile after you left and started roasting this as

153

soon as I got back. I think it's roasted long enough. I bought the bread."

She put the meat on a platter, placed it on the table. The gravy she poured in a bowl and added a small ladle. Two tin plates followed and some tin knives and forks. "Not the finest, but considering our surroundings, not too bad either." She used her apron again to take the bread and potatoes out of the oven.

"It'll do just fine."

They ate without much conversation, and it was good. Real good. Better even than what he'd had at the café. Marietta Manahan knew how to cook. The meal was topped off with hot bread smeared with plum preserves. Todd was afraid he'd have to let his belt out a notch. The only thing that wasn't perfect was his shorts. They were still damp and itching.

Finished, he complimented her on a fine meal, helped her gather the dirty dishes and stack them in the sink near the pump. "I'll wash them later, Doug. How about more coffee?"

Sipping coffee, sitting at the table, she said conversationally, "I learned to milk cows at home and I didn't much care for it, but I do miss fresh milk and butter. Only one man in White River has a milk cow and he sells butter for a big profit. If you want to go into business around here, the thing to do is import some milk cows. You could name your own price."

"I've done all the cow-milking I care to," he said with a grin. "But I'm like you, I miss the milk and cream."

"Did you have chickens on your farm? The farm where you were raised?"

"Yeah. Lost a lot of them to the coyotes, but my mother always kept a few."

154

"Are your folks still alive?"

When his face darkened and a frown appeared, she said quickly, "I'm sorry Doug. I didn't mean to pry."

"No," he sighed. "They're both dead."

"I'm sorry."

They sipped their coffee, and she forced a smile. "Well, I think I'd rather milk cows than be a saloon girl. I found out right quick I wasn't cut out for that kind of work."

"Yeah," he said, trying to smile with her, "that looks like it would be kind of hard to put up with."

"Oddly, it's not the miners and lumberjacks that are hard to take, it's the boss. He thinks everyone who works for him belongs to him."

"I've met a few bosses like that."

"We-el, no, Doug, being a man, you haven't. Not like J.D. Hays."

"Oh. You're right."

"In a way I admire the man. He came here with nothing but a wagonload of whiskey and built one of the finest saloons in the territory."

"I heard about that. Came from back east."

"St. Louis. Traveled through Kansas to Denver, heard about White River and spent his last dollar on a team and wagon and whiskey. Now look what he has."

Todd put his coffeecup down too quickly and it banged against the tabletop. "Through Kansas? When?"

"About a year ago, I think." Her green eyes studied his face. "Why, Doug? Is something wrong?"

CHAPTER SEVENTEEN

Todd's mind was racing. About a year ago. Through Kansas. "Miss Manahan—Marrie—did he talk to you much? I mean, did he ever tell you about his adventures?"

The green eyes probed, and she said flatly, "You came to White River looking for someone, didn't you, Doug?"

Had he ever mentioned it to the Manahan sisters? He wasn't sure, but he didn't think so. "Why did you say that?"

"It figures. You're no gambler and you're no prospector. And you're not looking for work. You're looking for something else."

She was wise to him. Any lie would arouse more suspicion. Forcing himself to relax, he picked up the coffeecup and took another sip. The coffee was lukewarm. "Aw, I was just curious. You know how it is. You hear about a boomtown where everybody is getting rich and you want to see it."

She was shaking her head before he finished talking. "I came here out of curiosity, but that's not what brought you here."

What could he say? He shrugged and said nothing.

"Do you think J.D. Hays could be the man you're looking for?"

His shorts itched and he squirmed in his chair, wishing he could go somewhere and take the damned things off and dry them out. And he wished he could avoid her questions. He mulled it over. Either lie or tell her to mind her own business. Which? Hell, a man couldn't be rude to a woman who'd just cooked him a fine meal.

"I doubt it. I think the man I was looking for is dead. Hooter Wilson was his name."

"But you're curious about Mister Hays."

Shrugging, he said, "Aw, maybe. A little."

"Want me to find out for you?"

"Huh? How would you find out?"

"He talks to me. Tell me what you want to know and I'll ask him."

"Just ask him, huh? And he'll tell you anything."

"And I won't go to bed with him either, if that's what you're thinking."

That's what he was thinking, but he couldn't admit it, and he was a little shocked at her frankness. "Why, that never entered my mind."

Here came that half-smile again. "You're not a very good fibber, Doug. I would understand if you thought that about me. The way I've behaved since I left home, anyone would get the wrong idea. My own sister asked some very pointed questions."

He squirmed in his damp shorts and drank the lukewarm coffee and kept his head down.

"What would you like to know about Mister Hays?"

Decision time again. Either answer her question or tell her to shut up. He met her gaze. The green eyes were serious. She was pretty. Not beautiful like her sister, but a good-looking girl.

"All right. I'd like to know if he was alone or traveling with somebody when he came through

158

western Kansas. Did he get into any gunfights? Did he survive an ambush? Things like that."

She put her elbows on the table and her chin in her hands. "You won't tell me why you want to know, will you?"

"No."

"I'll see J.D. Hays," she said with finality. "Now, shall I put the coffeepot back on the stove?"

"No thanks." Damn those shorts anyway. She was smiling at him. Did she guess he was wearing wet shorts? "I've had enough coffee to last a while. Sure was a good supper. Time for a gentleman to say good night."

He stood.

Standing too, she was still smiling. "Good night, Doug. I'll see you again. Soon."

"You won't get in any trouble with that Hays gent or his pet bear, whatsisname?"

"Don't worry. I'm a big girl."

He went to the door. "Well, good night."

Her smile was even wider. Damnit, if she had on damp underwear she wouldn't think it was so funny. Or did she think she was making him squirm?

"Good night, Doug."

The pack horse was better. After breakfast, Todd borrowed some beveled horseshoe nails and tools—a hoof rasp, nippers and a shoeing hammer—and pried the steel shoes off the horse's forefeet. He trimmed the feet and nailed the shoes back on, using the edge of the rasp to clinch the nails where they came out the side of the hooves. One at a time he picked up the feet of the bay horse and checked the shoes. The horse jerked its feet several times, but Todd managed to hang onto them. "Whoa, feller.

159

Whoa now." The shoes were good for a few more weeks. He led the pack horse outside the pen and walked him around for a while to unlimber the sore shoulder. The horse showed only a little lameness.

"Still want to trade 'im?" The stable owner leaned against a fence and yelled at Todd.

"Naw. He'll be ready to go this time tomorrow."

"Got my big brown horse back if you want to look at 'im."

"Naw. Reckon not."

"Let you have 'im for forty dollars boot."

"Naw. This one will do."

"He's a good stout horse. He can carry ever'thing you own and you too. And he'll stand tied anyplace. Let you have 'im for thirty dollars and that there horse."

"Naw."

"Let you have 'im for ten and that bay horse."

Todd walked over and grinned. "I wouldn't trade that bay horse for anything I've seen around here."

"He's a good-lookin' pony, all right. Where'd you get 'im? In Texas?"

"Yeah. Bought 'im off a mustanger. He was bigger than the rest of the horses he'd caught, but he was wilder than an outhouse mouse."

"Seem purty gentle now."

"I rode him most of the time when I helped trail a bunch of cattle to Wyoming. That'll gentle a colt. He can get on the other side of a steer faster than any horse I've ever rode."

"Trade you even. My big brown horse is what a travelin' man like you needs."

"Naw."

He sat on the bench in front of the livery barn and enjoyed the sun on his face. From there he could see the high ridge to the west where the snow glistened in the sun. A nice scene. He wondered what Marietta Manahan was doing. Was she visiting J.D. Hays? Was she in his office at the Gold Palace? Did he have a cot in there?

Aw, for crying out loud, just because she's got a wild streak and likes to do things most women won't do doesn't mean she's a whore.

Could J.D. Hays be the man he was looking for? Not likely. Too much the gentleman. A businessman. Knows how to get rich without robbing and killing.

Restless, he got up and walked. She'd said she'd see him soon, but didn't say exactly when or where. The longer the day was, the more restless he became. Should he go to her cabin, or just wait for her to come to him? Or what? By late afternoon he couldn't stand it anymore. He went to her cabin. Walked, spurs ringing.

No one answered his knock on the door. Around back, her dun horse grazed on the grass in the yard. Her saddle and outfit lay on the ground inside the three-sided stock shelter. Lay on its side with the skirts and stirrup leathers straight the way a cowboy would lay it. A washtub that he guessed substituted for a stock tank was nearly empty. Firewood was stacked against the wall near the one window. He remembered there was only one door and window to the cabin. The window was a small one. Well, that was enough, he reckoned.

Supper at the Denver Steak House was boiled beef and potatoes. He ate at the counter. The conversation around him was about somebody else striking it rich. Nothing about two men missing. Who the hell were those two? Just a couple of gunsels who happened along and saw a young woman alone? Or maybe they'd heard about the young woman living alone

161

and decided to have their pleasure with her. That wouldn't have happened in Texas. Men killed each other over nothing, but they didn't bother the women. Those two were men of no principle, pride, dignity or anything else. They might never be missed. Still, Marietta Manahan would have to tell the marshal about them.

She'd promised to leave Todd out of it. That was all that mattered.

He went back to his hotel, hoping she would try to find him there. He asked the clerk, manager or whatever he was to do him a favor. The man gave him the usual suspicious stare, but nodded.

"If a lady comes looking for me, tell her I'll be right back."

"We don't allow no . . ."

"Damnit, I'm not taking her to my room. Can't you say anything civil?"

Bristling, the clerk opened his mouth, then changed his mind and shut it. Todd was ready to tell him to take his damned hotel and put it where it couldn't be put. "You tell her what I said and you treat her like a lady, savvy?"

Nodding, the clerk swallowed a lump in his throat and kept quiet.

Again, no answer to his knock on her door. The horse was still cropping the grass in the back yard. The washtub had been half-filled with water. She had been back and left again.

The clerk shook his head in answer to his question. No one had been there looking for Douglas Brock. Damn. Waiting wasn't his favorite pastime, but that seemed to be all he could do. Unless . . .

The Gold Palace was crowded and noisy as usual. The bartenders were hard at work, and the piano player was banging on the keys, trying to make his music heard above the men's voices.

162

Pug Face, at the foot of the stairs, scowled menacingly. Todd worked his way to the bar and waited for Bob the bartender to notice him. Bob poured two shots of whiskey and a mug of beer for other customers and came over.

"Seen Miss Manahan tonight?"

"Yeah. She's here. Up there." Bob nodded toward the stairs.

"How long has she been there?"

"Most of the afternoon. Left for a while and came back."

"Oh." For some reason he didn't understand, a cloud of depression settled over him. She's spent most of the afternoon with that dandy and was with him now. Upstairs in his room.

"Wanta beer?"

"Yeah."

The voices, laughter, cursing, piano were all shut out of his mind as he drank the beer. What were they doing? Was she that kind after all? How could two sisters be so different? He glanced at the stairs. Pug Face gave him a smirk. He turned back to his beer mug and studied the yellow liquid. Looked like horse piss. The whole damned world looked like horse piss. To hell with everything and every damned body.

Get out of town, Todd Kildow, he told himself. Head west and keep going until he ran out of land. Forget everything. Forget his real name, who he was, where he came from, and don't ever think about where he was going. Yeah, he'd get that livery man out of bed if he had to, saddle up and git. If the pack horse was still lame, well . . . Well what?

He'd do something, anything, but git.

He turned to go, and shot one more glance at the stairs. He saw her.

CHAPTER EIGHTEEN

She looked like a whore, except she was better-looking than most. Her red hair was parted in the middle and combed down almost to her shoulders. Her lips were painted a bright red. She even had red spots painted on her cheeks. The dress she wore was, well, not what a lady would be caught dead in. Bright red. Some kind of shiny material. She didn't fill out the top as much as most of the saloon women, but she filled it enough. Her knees showed at the bottom. Small ankles. Net stocking.

A groan came out of Todd before he could stop it. He shook his head sadly.

All eyes turned to her. Even Pug Face watched her come down the stairs. Todd wanted to leave without being seen. He pulled his head down between his shoulders and moved toward the door.

"Doug. Doug, wait a minute." She had spotted him.

He stopped, turned and watched her walk toward him. Walked like a whore. Swung her hips. She smiled, and all that war paint made her smile kind of garish. Not pretty at all. He half expected her to ask him to buy her a drink.

She stopped before him, touched his arm. Everyone listened to what she had to say. She glanced

165

around nervously, licked her lips and said. "Douglas Brock, you old Texas longhorn, when're you gonna buy a lady a drink of whiskey?" Then in a whisper, she said, "Doug, it's not . . . I'll see you later, all right?"

When he tried to talk he almost strangled. "Uh, maybe some other time, Miss. Yeah, some other time. Got to go now."

She patted his arm, and there was as much push toward the door as pat.

Shoo. Now what the ring-tailed, bald-assed, slant-eyed hell?

Todd and the hotel clerk didn't speak to each other as he climbed the stairs. In his room, he pulled off his boots and lay back on the bed. He had a terrible urge to be gone. Horses could see very well in the dark, and by daylight they could be far away. White River and the Manahan sisters would be forgotten. Well, not entirely forgotten. He'd think about them from time to time, and he'd wonder what the younger one, the redhead, had been doing in J.D. Hays' office.

Yeah, he'd always wonder.

Well, now, come to think of it, she'd promised to ask that gentleman about his adventures on his way west. To do that she had to spend some time with him, didn't she? That didn't mean she was peeling off her clothes for him. She'd said she wasn't going to do that. Could she spend most of the day and part of the night with him without going to bed with him? Hell, who knows. And she did say she'd see Todd later. She was up to something, that was for sure.

See him later. That brought up the questions that had come up before. Where and when? Here at the hotel? At her cabin? What was he supposed to do, just wait? Wait here?

The wooden chair in the hotel lobby got more uncomfortable by the minute. He'd been sitting in it for at least three hours, off and on. Four times, he'd gone outside and stood in the dark on the sidewalk, looking toward the Gold Palace, hoping to see her coming. Now his hips ached from sitting in that damned chair.

Funny how a man could sit on a horse all day without feeling tired or cramped, but a few hours in a chair was hell. The ground would have been more comfortable. At least a man could stretch out on the ground. Damned chair. The clerk was dozing in another chair behind the counter, but he had a pillow under his ass. Did that yahoo ever go to bed?

Todd stood, stretched, rubbed his hips and went outside. No traffic. Everyone had gone to bed long ago. Everyone but the rowdies and gamblers in the saloons. He took a deep breath, shivered once, and leaned back against the building. Waited. Hell, he thought, this was foolish. He could stand here all night. Hell, he didn't know when he would see her again. If he ever did. He went back inside. Sat. It was a long night. Drowsy.

He awoke with a snort when she came in the door.

The clerk saw her first. His eyes took in her saloon-girl clothes, and he opened his mouth. "We don't . . ." Saw the scowl on Todd's face and shut his mouth.

"Miss Manahan." Todd wore a wry grin. "Imagine meeting you here."

Standing just inside the door, she shook her head. "I got away as soon as I could, Doug. Can we talk somewhere?"

"Sure." He took her arm and steered her out the door and onto the boardwalk. "What on earth, Miss Manahan, could we have to talk about?"

She spun around and faced him. Her mouth was tight. "You can cut out the sarcasm, Mister Douglas Brock. What the hell do you think I've been doing? Well, I'll tell you what I've been doing. I've been asking questions, holding off a man with six hands and a hungry look, and talking my way out of trouble. All for your benefit, Mister Douglas Brock, not mine."

"All right, all right." He shrugged. "I've been waiting for you. I apologize."

"Let's go to my cabin. I didn't learn much. In fact, I'm afraid the whole thing was for nothing. But I'll tell you what I did learn and maybe it'll mean something. I hope so."

"Miss Manahan. Marrie. I didn't want you to go to this much trouble for my benefit."

"Will you accompany me to my cabin, or are you ashamed to be seen with the likes of me?"

He could feel her green eyes on him in the dark. "Sure. Anything you say."

They didn't talk much. When she stumbled in her high-heeled slippers, he took her arm. At the cabin, he opened the door, took a match from a shirt pocket and struck it with a thumbnail. She waited in the door until he had a lamp lit, then came in and sat in a chair with her elbows on the table and her chin in her hands. She was shivering, so he built a fire in the cookstove and opened the oven door to let the heat out.

"You look beat, Miss Manahan. Marrie."

A crooked smile turned up one corner of her painted mouth. "To use some cowboy language, I feel like I've been shot at and missed, flung dung at and hit."

168

"You look it, too."

"The other side of her mouth turned up. "I look like a whore, don't I?"

"Well, I wouldn't say . . ."

"Yes, you would, if you were talking to another man. And I would too if I were in your place. Gawud, Doug, I never knew a man could have so many hands. For a while there, I thought he was going to put a gun to my head. I got away by telling him a lie about, well you know, the periods we women have to put up with."

"I wish you hadn't done it, Marrie. If I'd known, I wouldn't have allowed it." When a frown creased her forehead, he added, "I mean, I'd have tried to talk you out of it." He was relieved when the crooked smile returned. "Are you all right now? You ought to get to bed."

"I'm all right. Let me tell you what I found out. It's not much and probably won't help you."

"I appreciate your trying."

She wiped her mouth with the back of a hand, and her hand came away red. The lip rouge was now smeared. "First, I had to be careful, you know. I couldn't just fire questions at him. I had to pretend I was interested in going back to work at the Gold Palace, and I had to have a drink with him. Brandy. It tasted like fruit juice, but it was potent. Boy, was it ever. I tried to flatter him and said I admired a man who could start with so little and accomplish so much, and I asked him about his trip west from St. Louis. I said I'd heard that western Kansas was a terrible country with all kinds of robbers and killers and bloodthirsty Indians." She stood. "I'll put the coffee on."

"Let me do it." He pumped water into the coffee pot, found the sack of Arbuckles on a shelf and poured some into the pot. The fire was crackling and the oven was putting out some warmth now.

"Well, Doug, he didn't say anything at all about any trouble with white men. He did say he had some trouble with Indians."

"He did?" He sat across the table from her. "Was he by himself?"

"No, he was traveling with two other men when the Indians attacked and his two partners were killed."

He absorbed that, his eyes boring into hers. "Well, now, what do you know about that!"

Meeting his gaze, she said, puzzled. "A fight with Indians? I don't know why you're looking for somebody, Doug, but I'd have guessed it was over a fight with white men. Or a white man. Or a white woman."

He didn't hear her. His mind was working, moving possibilities around. Attacked by Indians. Two partners killed. Sure. Like hell. Of course he'd make up a story about how his partners were killed. Damn. Maybe it wasn't Hooter Wilson. Could it be . . . He was afraid to think about it. It would turn out to be just another disappointment. Another busted lead.

Yeah, just another false hope. Forget it.

"Doug? What are you thinking?"

"Aw nothing. Nothing at all."

"Yes you are. Something I said got your interest up." The green eyes had hold of his and wouldn't let go. "What is it? Tell me, Doug."

He didn't answer immediately. His mind was still working. An attack by marauding Indians left two of three partners dead. The third one got away. It could be true. The Cheyenne and Arapahoe hated the white-eyes. But it could be a made-up story too.

"Doug? Are you going to answer me?"

170

He'd have to find out. How? He couldn't ask Marietta Manahan to go back to the Gold Palace. How?

"Douglas Brock." Exasperation brought her features together in a tight bunch. "Talk to me. Now."

"Huh? Oh. All right." How much should he tell her? Not much. Not everything. "Marrie, you guessed right, I am looking for a man. For a while there I thought the man was Hooter Wilson, who is dead, but now I'm not so sure."

She had her chin in her hands, watching his face expectantly.

"The man I'm looking for was traveling with two others through western Kansas, and they killed some folks I know. Two of them were killed themselves in an ambush, but one got away. That's the one I'm looking for."

He hoped that was all he'd have to say. It wasn't.

"They murdered your mother and dad, didn't they Doug?"

"What? How did you . . . ?"

Shaking her head, she said, "It was a guess. Well, not entirely a guess. It was you, the way you carry a gun, as if you expect a fight. Your willingness to fight. Yet, you're an honest man, a man who was brought up in a good family. And there was your embarrassment at being asked questions about yourself and your plans. And the vague answers you gave about your folks. Plus the fact that you are obviously carrying a big worry. It adds up."

He kept quiet.

"There is one thing I haven't figured out." She waited for him to say something, and when he didn't, she went on. "Why are you hiding from the law?"

He didn't want to tell her.

"Oh." Her elbows came down from the table and

171

she sat up straighter in the chair. "I should have known. Three men killed your folks. Two of them were shot from ambush. You shot them."

Now he had his elbows on the table and his chin in his hands.

She talked on. "It happened in Kansas. Kansas is a state now with its own judicial system, local elections and civilization. It's a law-and-order state. The authorities there probably don't look kindly on a man who takes the law in his own hands. Is that it, Doug?"

No use denying it. She had it figured out. "Yeah." He looked down at the table.

"And for some reason or other you didn't get a good look at the man who got away from you. Was it dark? It had to have been dark."

Standing, she went to the stove and poured two cups of coffee, put one in front of him. He ignored it.

"I'm on your side, Doug."

"What?" He looked up then, "Why?"

A quick smile crossed her face, and in spite of the smeared paint, it was a handsome smile. "If you've learned anything at all about the younger Manahan sister, you know I like a challenge."

"Is that it? Another challenge?"

"No. I like you."

He believed her. As strange as she was, she was the kind to level with a man.

"Now," she said, taking a sip of coffee, "the question is, what are we going to do next?"

"We?"

"Sure. Like it or not, cowboy, you've got a partner. Me."

"A partner? A girl partner?"

"I have another question, Mister Douglas Brock. Partner." She smiled. "What is your real name?"

CHAPTER NINETEEN

The silence that followed was loaded. She waited for his answer. He had to decide how to answer. This girl was smart. She had everything figured out. Almost everything. He could lie to her, but he wouldn't fool her. She sat across the table, her green eyes fixed on his face, her lip rouge smeared. She reminded him of a clown he'd seen once in a tent show, and suddenly he had to chuckle.

"What if I told you my name is John Jones?"

"Huh-uh. That won't do."

"What if I told you my name is Todd Kildow?"

"That, I believe."

He picked up the coffeecup and took a sip. It was warm, but not scalding hot the way he liked it. "My dad was Isaac Kildow. My folks were farmers, but I've always liked cattle and horses, and I like land that's left the way nature made it."

"You had me fooled. I thought you were a real Texan."

"I worked in Texas."

Leaning back in her chair, she stretched her arms toward the ceiling. The red dress slipped down and showed a cleavage. He couldn't help staring. She ignored his stare.

"That makes you Texas enough. Gaw-ud, Todd, I

173

feel like I've been run over by a hay rake."

"You ought to get to bed. It's time for me to leave."
He drained his coffeecup and stood.

Standing too, she went to the sink and picked up a small mirror from the windowsill over the sink. A shriek came out of her. "My Gawd! Look at me! How long have I looked like this?"

He chuckled, but could think of nothing to say.

"I've got to take a bath, get out of this goshawful rag, get this paint off my face."

"I'll pump some water for you and than I'll go."

"I can pump my own water."

With a shrug of his shoulders, he said, "All right. Just thought I'd help a lady."

"A lady I'm not, but you can bring in that washtub from the back yard."

He went out, groped his way around the cabin, and found the tub in the dark. Back inside, he put it on the floor beside the stove. She'd taken a lid off the stove and placed a bucket of water over the open flame.

"Is there anything else I can do?" He could sure use a woman, and the more he looked at her the better she looked.

"No, Todd. Come back in the morning. We have to make some plans."

"Are you sure?"

The green eyes settled on him. "Yes."

"Well, then, good night."

"Good night, Todd."

He went to the door, opened it, looked back when she said, "Todd?"

"Yeah?" Maybe she'd changed her mind.

"You're not going to do anything foolish, are you? Like leaving town in the dark?"

He grinned a crooked grin. "Why? What would

174

you do?"

"Nothing. I won't betray you. But I hope you stick around. Maybe J.D. Hays is the man you're looking for. You don't want to leave town until we find out."

"I've been looking for a year. Another couple of days won't matter."

Smiling, still looking garish, she said, "That's what I wanted to hear. Good night, partner."

Rolling out of bed at daybreak was a habit that a few nights in a hotel couldn't break. Todd was up and feeding his horses long before the livery barn was unlocked. He found a short piece of rope and used it to lead his pack horse outside the pen and in a big circle. He even ran a hundred yards to get the horse to trot behind him. No sign of lameness. He could ride out anytime he wanted to.

He didn't want to.

The Denver Steak House was crowded with miners and sawmill workers getting ready for the early shift. He stood against a wall and waited until a stool at the counter was vacated. Breakfast was hotcakes and beefsteak. The café was out of pork, he was told.

Outside on the planks, he wondered what to do next. He'd been worrying about it all night and still hadn't decided. Marietta Manahan probably wouldn't be up yet. What would he do when she was up? Talk? She was a smart young woman. Maybe she could think of something.

Naw. Damned if he'd let a woman do his thinking for him.

All right then, what the ding-dang hell was he going to do? Go see J.D. Hays himself? Sure, why not. That gent didn't know anything about him. Wouldn't hurt to talk to the man. Probably wouldn't do any good either, but it wouldn't hurt.

He clomp-clomped down the plank sidewalk to the Gold Palace, and was happy to see Bob behind the bar.

"Doesn't this place ever close?" he asked.

"Nope. Business ain't exactly booming this time of day, and I'm the only bartender working, but we do take in a few bucks." Bob nodded in the direction of a gaming table where four men were playing cards. "Somebody has to carry likker to them. And over there"—he nodded at another table where a man sat with his face on the tabletop and his arms hanging straight down—"that boozehound usually wakes up this time of morning and wants to drink his breakfast."

Todd grinned. "Does he spend all his nights that way?"

"Purt' near. I hear he has a house somewhere, but he spends most of his time in here. He struck a vein last spring and sold his claim for enough bucks to keep him happy for a long time."

"If I slept that way I'd have a crick in my neck for the rest of my life."

Bob chuckled. "Oh, sometimes he goes around holding his head to one side, but he can sleep through most anything."

As if he knew they were talking about him, the man's head suddenly came up. He snorted, wiped a shirtsleeve across his eyes and squinted their way.

"Mornin' Mister Summers," Bob sang out.

"Hrrumph," the man said. He stood, rubbed his eyes and headed for a door in the back of the room.

"Don't you want to prime your pump first, Mister Summers?"

"Hrrumph."

Bob reached under the bar for a bottle of whiskey

176

and filled a shot glass. "He'll be back. Two shots, and then he'll go over to the steak house and stuff himself with coffee and flapjacks, and then he'll be back here."

Shaking his head with a chuckle, Todd allowed, "It would kill me to live that way."

"It'll prob'ly kill him too, but he'll die happy."

Sure enough, Mister Summers was back, picking up the shot glass. His hand shook so badly that he spilled some of the whiskey before he got the glass to his mouth. "Aaaah." Then he went into a coughing fit while Bob filled the glass again. Coughing subsided, finally, he drank the second glassful in one gulp, and looked around with bloodshot eyes. He focused on Todd.

"Ain't I seen you before?"

"Could be. I've been in here before."

The rheumy eyes went to the Remington and back to Todd's face. "Now I recollect. You're the cowpuncher that stared down old Hank." The wrinkled face with a week's growth of gray whiskers screwed up in thought. "That was a week ago, wasn't it? How come you're still walkin' around?"

Bob answered, "It was only a couple of nights ago, Mister Summers."

The man flicked a hand. "No matter. You're the onliest one I ever seen talk back to old Hank and live to brag about it."

"I'm not bragging," Todd said. "He scared the hound-dog hell out of me."

"Scared you, huh?" The eyes squinted closer. "A scared man that don't show it is a dangerous man. Pour me another'n, Bob."

The drink was poured, downed. Another coughing fit, and, "Have one on me. Any man that can face old Hank is a man I wanta call friend."

177

"No thanks. One beer is all I need this early."

"How about some coffee, then? Time for my mornin' constitutional."

"I've had breakfast. Thanks anyway."

"You got somethin' else to do?"

"No. Can't say I have."

"Come on along, then. I'll buy you some coffee."

Todd looked at Bob. Bob shrugged.

"Why not? I can use another cup of java."

The café was no longer crowded, but dirty dishes were stacked everywhere. The middle-aged waitress looked as if she was ready to drop but she managed a smile when she saw who came in the door. "Mornin', Mister Summers."

They sat at the counter, and she quickly cleared the dirty dishes away. "Your usual, Mister Summers?"

"Hrrumph."

The coffee was hot and black and good. Todd sipped his with pleasure. Summers gulped a swallow, wiped tears from his eyes and gulped down another swallow.

Todd waited for the other man to speak, not knowing what to say.

"You sellin' cattle?"

"Naw. I just came up here to see what all the excitement is about. I hear men are getting rich digging up gold."

"Some are. I did. But I knew what I was doin'. Some a these jaspers wouldn't know gold or silver if it bit 'em on the ass."

"That's why I'm not up there digging."

"The smart ones buy up the good claims and haul in a steam engine and build a headframe and go to diggin' ore by the ton. They hire somebody else to do the work."

"I hear they buy some good claims pretty cheap."

A deep-throated chuckle came from Summers.

178

"Yeah, but I ain't that dumb. I got a good price and put the money in the bank. Alls I have to worry about is if the damn bank don't go broke."

Shrugging, Todd said, "What else can a man do? You can't carry it around in your pockets."

A platter of ham and eggs was placed on the counter in front of Summers, and he dug into it with a bent fork.

"Say." Todd looked up at the waitress. "I thought you were out of . . . aw, never mind."

Summers ate silently, and when he was finished, he belched, took another gulp of coffee and said, "Speakin' of the bank, I got to get over there. No tellin' how much I owe the Gold Palace and this here restaurant. Got to get some a my money out."

Trying to joke, Todd said, "Better get it out before these hardcases around here beat you to it."

"Some a them tried, and they're dead."

"Yeah, I heard about that. I heard they didn't get twenty feet out the door."

"I know it. I was there."

"You were there?"

"Yup. I know stuff about that robbery that most folks don't know. I know—knew—the robbers. One a them, anyways."

Todd studied the contents of his coffeecup. "Did you happen to know a gent by the name of Hooter Wilson?"

"Shore. Knowed 'im well. It was his big mouth that got 'im killed. Shot off his mouth to too many people."

"Oh? Like who?"

"Like that Mister Hays, the gent that owns the Gold Palace."

"Do you think J.D. Hays warned the bank guards?"

The stubbled face turned his way. Its breath

179

smelled like something dead. "You're full of questions, ain't you?"

Forcing a grin, Todd answered, "Yeah, I've got a hell of a curiosity."

"Alls I can say is him and old Hays got drunker'n a tumblebug one night, and it was the next day that Hooter and that other feller got shot. Them messengers was waitin' for 'em."

Todd was staring at the bottom of his coffeecup. He spoke mostly to himself. "You don't say?"

"Wa-al, I got to git over to the bank. Whenever I see you at the Gold Palace again, I'll buy you a drink of whiskey."

"Wait a minute. Is Hays the kind of gent who would turn on a friend?"

"Alls I can say is he's got a sneaky way about 'im. He ain't the gentleman he 'pears to be."

Todd didn't look up as Summers left. A question was running through his mind:

Why would Hays want a drinking pal killed?

CHAPTER TWENTY

It worried him as he went out on the street, back to the livery barn, back to his hotel. He paid for another night's stay at the hotel and counted his money. Soon he'd have to move out of the hotel, sleep on the ground, and stake his horses out on the free grass. Or get a job. Maybe he could get a job at a sawmill. It surely didn't take much experience to roll logs or carry lumber. He'd have to get some low-heeled shoes. These boots wouldn't do for that kind of work. Better save enough money to buy a pair of shoes. Or saddle up and ride on.

No, he couldn't ride on now. It was getting interesting around White River. He'd stay a little longer even if he had to find a job working on foot. Yeah, get a job and hang around the Gold Palace long enough, and no telling what else he might hear. In a couple of days, he'd look for a job.

Right now, though, he wanted to talk to Marietta Manahan again. Maybe she'd heard something about J.D. Hays and his drinking spree with Hooter Wilson, something she didn't know was important.

He walked the three blocks to her cabin and knocked on the door. No answer. He went around back and saw her dun horse and the washtub half-full of water. After standing near the front door a few

181

minutes, he walked back to the livery barn, and that's where he found her. She was leaving the barn and coming his way. Didn't look at all like the girl he'd visited last night. Didn't look like the mannish sloppy girl he'd first seen at a mountain cabin. She was wearing that dress again, the one that was tight from the waist up but billowy from the waist down, the kind of long dress that most women wore. Her sorrel hair was parted in the middle and combed down to her shoulders. He grinned when he saw her. She could fix herself up more different ways than anyone he'd ever known. Not beautiful like her sister, but pretty.

"Mornin' Miss, uh, Marrie."

"Morning, Todd. I've been looking for you." Barely visible under the bottom of her dress were the lace-up, flat-heeled shoes.

"I was looking for you."

"Want to talk?"

"Yeah. You're not dressed for sitting on the ground. Where . . . ?"

"I can sit on the ground. This dress is washable."

They found a spot behind the pens, a spot where they had sat in the dark one recent night.

"What would you like to talk about?" She folded her legs under her.

"I was wondering if . . . Let me tell you what I heard this morning." He sat cross-legged, facing her, and told about his conversation with Summers.

Her eyebrows arched. "Boy, that's something to think about, isn't it?"

"Yeah, that opens up possibilities."

"It sure does. Are we thinking the same thing? I mean, do you think the late Hooter Wilson was con man enough to get J.D. Hays to spill his secrets?"

"Uh-huh."

182

"And Mister Hays, when he sobered up, could have realized he'd told Hooter Wilson something he should have kept to himself."

"Uh-huh."

"But not to worry. He had a way to be sure Mister Wilson didn't let it go any further."

"Yep. All he had to do was whisper the right words in the right ear, and Hooter Wilson's lips were sealed forever."

"And no suspicion on him."

"Nope. He's still the gentleman businessman."

"Boy oh boy." She put her elbows on her knees and made a steeple of her fingers. "Now, what we have to do is find out what Mister Hays told Mister Wilson."

"And that"—Todd straightened his legs and recrossed them—"won't be easy."

Horses in the pens were rearing and biting playfully at each other, but the man and woman didn't notice.

"Hmm." Her chin was in her hands now. "You're right about that. He let it slip once and he won't make that mistake again."

"And if he'd told somebody else, that somebody would be dead too."

"Or a long way from here. Or bribed. Or . . . well, there's Hank. J.D. Hays and Hank are pretty close. Hank might know."

"He won't tell. I'd bet anything on that."

"You're right. Hank won't tell."

Silence. Except for a steam whistle somewhere and a freight wagon creaking past on the road.

"Well." She sighed. "There's only one way."

He looked at her expectantly.

"I'm going back to the Gold Palace."

"Oh no. I can't let you do that."

The red eyebrows arched again. "Can't let me? It's

183

been a long time since anybody *let* me do anything."

He leaned forward, closer to her. "Now listen here, Marrie, you looked like a wrung-out dishrag when you got out of there last night, and this time he won't take no for an answer. Besides, you wouldn't learn anything anyhow."

"I might. Now that I know exactly what you're looking for, I can ask the right kind of questions."

"And get hurt. Or worse . . ."

"Got a better idea, Todd?"

"No. Not now. I'll think of something."

Leaning back with her hands on the ground behind her, she said, "All right, go ahead. Think of something."

"I'll tell you one thing I'm thinking. I'm thinking it won't do any good anyhow. What if he does get tanked up on liquor or passion or something and tells you everything? He'll deny it later."

That brought on another long silence. She straightened her legs. The boys' shoes looked out of place with the cotton dress. Finally, she said, "Let's start at the beginning, Todd, and decide what we want to do—need to do—and then try to figure a way to do it."

"All right."

"Tell me, you've been looking for a year now for one of the men who murdered your folks. Surely you have some kind of plan of action in case you find him."

"No." A long sigh came out of Todd. "I have no plan. I reckon I've been hoping for a miracle."

"If you could have your wish, what kind of miracle would you wish for?"

Another sigh. "I could kill him and get my revenge."

"That might make you feel better, but it wouldn't

184

solve your problem."

"No, there's only one way. That's to find the man and get him to go back to Kansas with me and admit everything."

"And you believe the sheriff and the prosecutor would then absolve you of wrongdoing."

His answer was weak. "It's . . . it's the only way."

"Boy." Leaning forward, she put her chin in her hands again. "Well, I wanted a challenge."

He said nothing.

"You're right. It will take a miracle."

Glumly, he said, "Yeah."

Suddenly, she jumped up and brushed the dirt off the seat of her dress. "As you cowboys always say, you can't do a damned thing if you don't try."

"You're not going back there?" He stood and faced her.

That half-smile again. "My dad once told me that if I had a brain it would rattle like a pea in a barrel. Well, I'm completely brainless and mule-headed to boot. Haven't you heard?"

"If you got hurt or . . . or anything, I'd have a low opinion of myself for the rest of my life."

"I hereby release you from all blame. We're partners, aren't we?"

"No. No, we're not partners. I don't want a partner who ain't got any better sense than to do what you're thinking about doing."

The smile vanished. "Don't worry, Todd. I can run like an antelope." Then the smile was back. "On second thought, go ahead and worry. It's good to know you care."

All he could do was stutter and stammer.

"Tell you what, why don't you wait for me in my cabin. That way I'll know where to find you."

"Wait for you? Like hell."

185

"Wait for me, please. That's the first time I've said please since I was a child. Will you wait for me, Todd?"

"Huh," he snorted.

She turned to go. Stopped and spoke one more word: "Partner."

Todd had done all the waiting he wanted to do. Seemed that's what he'd done most since coming to White River. Wait. Kill time. No, by God, he wasn't about to sit in her cabin and wait.

He saddled his bay horse and rode out of town, leading the pack horse. He crossed the river and went on a few miles; then, satisfied that the pack horse was no longer lame, he went back to the livery barn. After a beef sandwich at the Denver Steak House, he walked aimlessly. He walked past the Buckhorn saloon, turned and went back.

"Beer," he said. It was served. Not many people. Only two tables were occupied. He spotted the blond woman he'd accompanied to a cabin in back, but she ignored him. She thought he was crazy. Maybe she was right. No one to talk to in there. He wondered which of the two women friends Hooter Wilson had slept with the night before he was killed. This one? Hell, ask. What was her name? Come to think of it, he didn't know.

"Miss," Todd said, approaching her end of the bar. "Can I buy you a shot of whiskey or something?"

With a shrug of her almost bare shoulders, she said, "Why not?"

Four seconds later, the drink was poured and downed. Todd paid.

"Can I ask you something else?"

"All you want to do is ask questions. Well, ask. As long as you keep the liquor coming."

186

"It's about Hooter Wilson."

"Could of guessed. That's all you wanta know about."

"Did he spend the night with you before he was killed?"

"No. I waited up for him but he didn't come."

"Thanks."

"That's all you wanted to know?"

"Yeah, I think so."

She rolled her eyes and, with a forefinger, drew an imaginary circle around her right temple.

He didn't finish his beer. It was warm anyway.

Walking on the plank walk, stepping aside for other pedestrians, he remembered one of Wilson's women saying he liked to talk, gamble and drink, but when it was bedtime he had to have a woman. If it wasn't the blond one at the Buckhorn then it must have been the one named Lilly at the Gold Palace. He went there. No Lilly. Too early. Bob the bartender was putting on his jacket.

"Time for a shift change," Bob said. "Ain't payday anywhere so the place won't be so busy tonight. I get to take the night off."

"What do you do on your night off?"

"Get a good steak supper. Some sleep. Come back. Find a woman. First, though, I might load my old six-shooter and help hunt for that Indian."

"What Indian?"

"The one that's been prowling around here at night. Somebody spotted him out behind this building last night. I always wanted to shoot an Indian."

"He might shoot back, you know."

"Don't think he's got a gun."

Todd knew the Indian had a gun. Two guns. But

he kept it to himself.

"When does Lilly usually show up?"

"Couple of hours."

He could go over to Marietta Manahan's cabin and try again to talk her out of going back to the Gold Palace. Naw. He'd tried and it didn't work.

The livery man was forking hay from a wagon with no sideboards to a huge stack next to the barn. The hay was meadow grass that had been cut and hauled to town. Todd sat on a pole fence a while, went to the café and had a steak, went to his room to count his money. Two more days, and he'd be broke. He'd have to work at a sawmill or in a mine. He didn't think he could stand to be under the ground.

The Gold Palace was doing business, but it wasn't as loaded as he'd seen it. That was good. Lilly was drinking and talking with a miner who wore a full beard and a striped broadcloth shirt. Damn. He had to talk to her, but he didn't want to buy a drink for himself and her too. He'd have to just stand around until she was free. He went over to the roulette table and watched. Only two men were playing. They both swore a blue streak when the wheel stopped spinning. Hank was in his usual place.

Marietta Manahan came in.

"Oh Lord," Todd groaned. She was wearing that red dress again. Half-dress. And that godawful paint. Her eyes fell on Todd, but she showed no recognition and walked past him to the stairs. Hank stopped her, and they talked in a low tone. Then he stepped aside and she went up the stairs.

Todd watched her. At the top, she paused, half turned and shot him a glance. Her face was expressionless. Todd watched her disappear into an upstairs hall, and continued staring after her. He was worried. Almost sick with worry. A small hand touched his arm, and he looked into the face of Lilly.

"Buy me a drink?"

"Oh, uh, sure."

At the bar, he kept looking back at the stairs, hoping to see her coming down. He paid for the colored water without ordering a drink for himself.

"Something the matter?"

"Huh? Oh. Naw." He had to forget her. "Let me ask you something. About Hooter Wilson."

"Oh, him again. I told you everything I know about him."

"Did he sleep with you the night before he was killed?"

"Yeah. So what?"

"Did he tell you anything abut a conversation with J.D. Hays?"

"Naw. He was so drunk all he did was pull off his boots and fall on the bed and pass out."

"That's all?"

"Yeah. Funny. You're the second man to ask me about this."

"Oh? Who else?"

"I'm dry again."

The bartender was right there. Todd paid. "Who else?"

"Him." She nodded at Hank.

"He asked the same thing I just asked?"

"Yeah, and he really wanted to know. I had a hell of a time making him believe me. In fact, he . . . he hurt me."

"He did, huh? How?"

"He tore my clothes off, and . . . I'll tell you all about it, but it'll cost you some money."

"Does he like to hurt women?"

"That's the only way he can get satisfied."

Todd was no longer listening. His blood had turned cold. Fear was in his throat. Hank was not in his usual spot. Hand was nowhere to be seen.

A woman's scream came from upstairs.

Todd was running for the stairs, his hand on the butt of the Remington.

Running as fast as he could.

CHAPTER TWENTY-ONE

He paused when he reached the foot of the stairs. It flashed through his mind that he would be a perfect target on the stairs. Anyone shooting from the second floor hall couldn't miss. But he had to get up there.

The Remington was in his hand now and the hammer was back. It was either creep up the stairs slowly, watchfully, or run up and get to the top as fast as possible. He started up carefully, watching the top, six-gun ready. She screamed again.

Now he was running, taking two steps at a time, making more noise than he wanted to, but knowing he had to get up there. A quick blur of a man crossed the hall above him, a wide-shouldered man. Todd let loose a shot without taking aim, wanting to get off the first shot. The Remington bucked in his hand, and he thumbed the hammer back, ready to shoot again.

The broad-shouldered man disappeared, but Todd knew he wasn't hit. All he could hope to do was to keep the man from stepping out into the hall and taking aim.

At the top, he stopped, breathing in shallow breaths, eyes straining to catch any movement. There were three doors on each side of the hall. One of them, two doors ahead and on his right, was open.

The only sound was a woman's sobs. Floorboards creaked as he moved past the first door. His eyes were on the open one. Damn floor. They knew exactly where he was and he didn't know where they were.

He kept the Remington up at eye level. He would have to shoot fast. Fast and accurate.

It was a bad spot to be in, and he knew it. An icy chill swept over him, and the hair on the back of his neck tingled. He didn't dare take his eyes off the open door, and while he was watching that, someone could pop out of a door behind him, or come up the stairs, and blow his head off with a shotgun.

One more door between him and the open one. Todd put his back to the wall as he inched toward it. Stopping there, he listened. All he could hear was the woman's sobs. Marietta Manahan. Hurt. And the men who had hurt her were waiting for him. Waiting for a chance to kill him.

The sobbing stopped, and it was quiet. His back to the wall, Todd inched past the closed door, ready to whirl around and shoot if the door opened.

She was in the next room. Had to be. That's where the sobbing had come from. Now it was quiet.

Then she groaned. A strangled painful groan. The kind of groan that a human tries to hold back but can't. Another. They were hurting her again.

He had to get in there and stop them. He had to do something and he had to do it now. He steeled himself, ready.

No.

That's what they wanted. They wanted him to rush in and make a target of himself. They were waiting. It would be suicide to run in there.

She screamed, "Todd, he's behind the door. He's behind the . . ." Her screams were cut off. Someone had clamped a hand over her mouth.

He stepped away from the wall to where he could

see the open wooden door. Wide open. A man could be hiding behind it. Probably was.

But where was she? He couldn't just jump in there and scatter lead without knowing where Miss Monahan was.

She yelled again, "I'm over here. Over . . ." Again, she was cut off.

Now he knew. She was not behind the door.

He fired three shots, each one making a splintery hole about a foot apart. The booming of the Remington hammered his ears. And then it was quiet again.

A spooky kind of quiet.

Slowly, the door moved a few inches. Something hard and metallic clattered to the floor. Something else, soft and heavy, thudded to the floor.

Todd jumped into the room, eyes wild, ready to shoot.

J.D. Hays had a silver-plated revolver in his hand, but when he found himself looking up the bore of the Remington, he dropped it. His hands shot into the air as if they'd been yanked up on strings.

"Don't shoot, don't shoot."

Still fearful, still feeling that chill and that prickling on the back of his neck, Todd looked behind him. A man was face-down on the wooden floor. His arms were outstretched, and a Colt six-shooter was on the floor a foot away from his right hand. Todd stepped back and gave the gun a kick. It went skittering. The man didn't move.

J.D. Hays kept his hands in the air. Marietta Manahan was sitting on the floor. Her sorrel hair was down over her eyes, and the paint on her face was smeared.

Todd groaned when he saw her. Anger quickly

193

replaced the chill in his blood. She was tied hand and foot. The red dress was torn down to here waist, and her round, pink-tipped breasts were exposed. Her eyes were downcast, as if she was ashamed of her nudity. He holstered the Remington and reached into his left pocket for the folding knife he always carried. He squatted before her.

"Marrie?" he said.

She looked up then.

And her eyes widened and another scream tore out of her, "Behind you, Todd."

Oh lord. He should have known, should have been more careful. He'd made a bad mistake.

The man on the floor wasn't Hank.

Hank spoke harshly, "Stand up, cowboy, I want you to see it coming."

Afraid to breathe, Todd stayed perfectly still, squatting on his heels.

J.D. Hays let his hand drop to his sides, and a wicked smile spread across his face. "Shoot him. Shoot the son-of-a-bitch."

Todd figured his chances. Zero to none. Hank was behind him, had him in his gunsights. Todd was on his heels. The Remington was in its holster on his right hip.

"Stand up, tough man. Watch yourself die."

Hank liked to hurt women. Maybe he liked to tease men before he killed them. That could be his undoing. Todd knew Hank was directly behind him. Had to be in the doorway. If only he could . . .

Marietta Manahan was crying softly. "I'm sorry, Todd. I'm sorry."

Todd's mind screamed. NOW! DO IT NOW!

He threw himself to the left, hit the floor on his left

shoulder, rolling. The Remington was in his hand. The hammer was back. A gun crashed like a clap of thunder and a lead slug tore into the floor beside him. Todd fired twice without taking aim, fired at a hulk in the doorway.

Raised the gun to eye level, intending to make the last bullet count.

It wasn't needed.

The broad-shouldered Hand had a surprised look on his face, a look that changed to one of shock. His right arm was so heavy he couldn't hold it up, and when the Colt boomed a second time the slug hit the floor between Hank's feet.

Todd was looking down the barrel of the Remington, ready.

But the saloon bouncer had two bullet-holes in him—one in the stomach and the other in the middle of the chest. First it was his knees that buckled, then his eyes rolled up into his head, and he collapsed like a wet rag.

Another warning yell came from the girl. "Todd!"

He spun around to see J.D. Hays kneeling and reaching for the silver-plated revolver on the floor. Immediately, the Remington was aimed at a new target.

Hays jumped up as if he were on a spring, and again his hands jerked toward the ceiling. "Don't shoot."

Through clenched teeth, Todd muttered, "You son-of-a-bitch." The Remington was aimed at a spot between the saloon owner's eyes.

"Please don't shoot. Please." The man was on the verge of tears. "I'll give you some money." His body was shaking, and his voice was hysterical. "It's in my desk. Just let me reach in my desk and I'll give you some money. Don't shoot me, please."

195

Todd hissed, "You goddamned son-of-a-bitch." His finger tightened on the trigger.

"Please."

The trigger finger halted. Something pulled at the back of Todd's mind. He tried to push it away, but it persisted. What was it? The man wasn't fit to live. No jury would convict him of killing a woman-raper. Hell, there was no jury in White River anyway. There wasn't even a lawman right now. Kill the son-of-a-bitch.

No, wait.

J.D. Hays could be the man he'd been looking for. He couldn't prove anything if the man was dead.

All right. But first he had to take care of Marietta Manahan. The girl was sniffing, but not crying.

"Down on the floor," Todd ordered. "If you want to live, you'll get down on your belly. Do it, damnit."

It took a second for Hays to understand, and then he dropped to the floor like a sack of flour.

"Don't move. Move and you're dead."

Todd collected the three revolvers from the floor, stuck them in his belt and went to the girl. He had to holster the Remington again to reach the folding knife in his pocket, open it and cut the ropes that bound her. She kept her eyes down as she stood, rubbing her wrist. Suddenly she realized she was half naked, and she pulled up the torn dress and held it over her breasts.

"Let's get out of here," Todd said, leading the way to the door. To the man, he said, "Don't move til we're long gone. If you do you'll join your hired men in hell."

They went down the stairs, the girl in the lead, holding her dress up with both hands. Todd tried to watch the top of the stairs and the crowd below at the same time. The three pistols in his belt were heavy, and one slipped out and fell to the carpeted stairs. He left it there. Men and women below had heard the shots, but hadn't moved. They remained frozen as Todd and Miss Manahan made their way through the long room to the door.

Finally, someone asked, "What happened up there, mister?"

"Hank and another man are dead and J.D. Hays is a sniveling coward," Todd said. "We're leaving, and it would be dangerous to try to stop us."

No one tried, and they were out the door and onto the planks. Todd holstered the Remington and threw the other guns into some weeds between two buildings.

Man and woman didn't speak as they walked with quick steps to her cabin. He struck a match and started to light a lamp. Then she spoke.

"Don't. Leave it dark."

"Why?"

"I have to change clothes, that's why."

"Oh."

He heard cloth rustle, heard the clomp of heavy shoes on the wooden floor. Then she struck a match and lit a lamp herself. She was dressed in the baggy overalls with a wool shirt. Her Winchester rifle was standing in a corner of the room. Without a word, she grabbed it, jacked the lever down to make sure it was loaded, and headed for the door.

"Hey, wait a minute! Where're you going?"

"To kill that son-of-a-bitch." She yanked the door open.

"Hey, wait a minute!" He grabbed her from behind before she could get out the door. Grabbed her around the waist.

"Let me go." She hung onto the rifle, but jumped, kicked, twisted, and grunted with exertion.

"Marrie, hold on now. Just hold on a minute."

She was half crying now with anger and frustration. "I've got to kill the son-of-a-bitch."

"I know. I'd feel the same way. I almost killed him myself. But I need him alive, Marrie. I think he's the man I've been looking for."

She stopped struggling. He let go his hold on her and shut the door. When she turned to him tears were running down her rouge-smeared face.

"I'm just so goshdamned mad. I'm so goshdamned tired of being treated like a second-class citizen. Women have no rights at all. This country went to war to set the Negroes free, and we women are nothing but slaves ourselves. We're not even allowed to vote. Men think they can do anything they want with us. We're supposed to take off our clothes and lie down to please the goshdamned men."

For a second, he thought of reminding her that she went to the Gold Palace knowing what might happen, but saying something like that wouldn't be smart at all. And when he thought about it, she ought to have the right to go where she wanted and do what she wanted without some yahoo trying to force her down and rip her clothes off.

What was the world coming to, anyway?

All he could do was shrug.

She stomped over to her cot, laid the rifle down and sat with her hands on her knees and her chin in her hands. He could see she was struggling to bring her anger under control. Finally, she looked up. Her face was still streaked.

"All right, so both times that man tried to . . . to rape me, other men came to the rescue. You're not all bad. But goshdamn it, Todd, I'm so sick of being treated this way."

He shrugged again and said nothing.

"All right, you've heard me cuss, and you've seen me half-naked. What do you think of the younger Manahan sister now?"

"Well, there are some words I'd rather not hear you say, but if you feel like cursing, go ahead."

"Sometimes I feel like it, and this is one of those times. I'm so goshdamned sick of being treated like some kind of inferior animal just because I happen to be female." Her voice turned bitter, and she mimicked, "You can't do this and you can't do that. Well, some damned day we women are going to do something about it! You'll see. And I'm gonna do my part."

He pulled a chair away from the table and dropped into it. "Can't say I blame you Marrie. I'd feel the same way."

She looked at the floor between her feet. Then she wiped her eyes with the palms of her hands and looked up. A forced smile turned up one corner of her mouth. "I owe you, Todd. I owe you a lot."

"Naw." He shrugged again.

"Yes, I do. Here I am feeling sorry for myself and you've got problems too. What was it you said about Jackass Hays being the man you're looking for?"

"Well." Todd shifted in his chair. "I talked to Lilly again at the Gold Palace, and it's for sure old Hays said something to Hooter Wilson he wished he hadn't. He sent Hank to her to find out if he'd repeated it to her."

"What do you suppose he said?"

"It could have been something about a double murder in western Kansas."

She was thoughtful. "Yes, it could have been. But how can we prove it?"

"That," he shook his head sadly, "is one h—heck of a problem. I just flat don't know."

"The marshal would be no help."

"No. But one thing did come into my mind up there in that room. Hays is a coward. He's scared of being killed. Or even hurt. If he thought his life was in danger he'd do anything."

"So you think maybe if we poked a gun up his nose he'd cry like a baby and tell everything."

"He might. I don't know what else to do."

Suddenly her shoulders slumped and she looked at the floor again. "You had your chance. Just a little while ago. You had him ready to do anything to stay alive. But you were more concerned about me." Looking up, she was half smiling and half crying. "Todd, do you know something?"

"What?"

"You're crazy!"

CHAPTER TWENTY-TWO

Marietta Manahan stood, went to the kitchen sink and pumped a washpan of water. She looked at her reflection in the small mirror on the windowsill and let out another shriek.

"Todd, turn your head."

"What? Why?"

"Don't look at me. I'm, a mess."

"Don't look at you? I've been looking at you."

"Don't look at me anymore until I wash my face."

"Aw, all right, if it'll make you happy." He turned his chair so it was facing the opposite wall.

Water splashed. She said, "Brrr." Four minutes later, she said, "You can turn around now." Her face was clean and her hair was combed.

Todd's eyes went over her, from the sorrel hair to the baggy overalls to the boys' lace-up shoes. He had to chuckle.

"What's so funny?"

"You. You don't want to be seen with your face dirty, but you don't care about . . ."

"About my clothes? These are working clothes. They're more comfortable and they allow more freedom of movement than a dress. All right?"

Still chuckling. "All right. Like your sister said, you're a strange one."

"I know I'm strange. But I make sense, don't I? Why should we women be forever tripping over dresses?"

He didn't answer, but instead mused, "What's the world coming to?"

Then his eyes fell on the red dress where it had been thrown on the floor, torn and dirty, and his smile vanished. The vision of her with the dress down around her waist made his face warm, and he was embarrassed by the thought that went through his mind.

"I'd better go."

"Don't go."

"Well, I can't . . ." His gaze went to the narrow cot, to her. "I can't stay here all night." He was thinking again of her bare breasts.

Somehow, she read his thoughts, and her face turned red. "No, no, not that." She hugged herself and shivered. "I can still feel their hands on . . . no, Todd. Can't we just talk? I won't lie to you, Todd. I'm not a virgin." Her hands fluttered nervously. "You know me, I have to try everything—once. But that was all."

"Listen, it's none of my business."

"Yes it is. I want you to know."

"Why?"

"Because. That's all. Just because."

Sitting again, he said, "If that's what you want, but it's going to be a long night."

"I'll put some coffee on. We have to make some plans anyway."

While she built a fire in the cookstove and readied the coffeepot, he shook his head in disbelief. Sometime in the future, he'd tell somebody about this, and that somebody would think he was just making up a story. Hell, he grinned to himself, he wouldn't believe it either.

They talked. Talked and drank coffee.

A plan of action wouldn't take form. What they had to do, they decided, was to get J.D. Hays alone somewhere, threaten him with death and get him to confess everything. But the problem was how to do it. And there were other problems. His confession would mean nothing unless it was witnessed. It wouldn't do any good to take Hays back to Kansas. He would change his story once he was out of danger. The witness would have to go to Kansas too.

She said, "I'd be a witness, of course, but I wonder if that would be enough."

"Probably not."

"The prosecutor would tell the jury we were lovers and I should be expected to lie for you."

"Too bad we can't get a church pastor or somebody like that in on this."

"How about a deputy U.S. marshal?"

"Sure. The marshal will stand around with his hands in his pockets and watch me force a confession out of J.D. Hays."

The coffeepot was empty. Todd stood and stretched. That cot looked mighty good. She crossed her arms on the table and put her head on her arms.

"Why don't you lie down, Marrie?"

Her voice was muffled. "If you can stay up, I can stay up."

"I'm not so sure I can stay up."

"Then you lie down."

"Yeah, I know, you can do anything a man can do."

Her head came up, and her green eyes were weary. "I don't make that claim anymore. Not after what's

203

happened the last few days. But I can pull my weight." She put her head down again.

"Sure."

At daylight, she went out to see her horse while he went to the livery barn to throw some hay to his horses. Then they ate breakfast together. She had some cured ham, and she made good flapjacks. Neither of them could stand the thought of more coffee.

He told her about his sorry financial condition, and said he'd have to move out of the hotel and take his horses out of the livery pens.

"What will you do, Todd?"

"I don't know. I'm going to have to do something soon."

"I'll lend you some money. Come to think of it, I owe you some money for going back to my mountain cabin with me. I promised to pay you, remember?"

"Naw. Wonder when the marshal will get back?"

"I don't know. Why?"

"As soon as he gets back I'm going to have to get him and J.D. Hays together and get Hays to talk." His faded blue eyes locked onto her green ones. "I've been thinking about this, Marrie. I'm not hiding from the law anymore. I've got money in the bank in Kansas and I've got property there, and I'm going back one way or the other."

Her gaze met his and her voice was sincere. "I've been thinking about it too. I'm going with you."

"Huh?" What was this girl going to say next? Or do?

"If you'll let me."

"Let you? I thought nobody could let you do anything?"

204

"You could."

"Huh?"

That half-smile again. "You think about it, Todd. In the meantime, let's go see if the marshal is back."

"Maybe I'd better go alone. When I tell him who I am he'll arrest me. I only hope he'll listen to me and ask questions of J.D. Hays."

"You're right. You'll need a friend outside."

Putting on his hat, he headed for the door. "Wish me luck."

"Good luck, partner."

He had to wait until the stage arrived at mid-afternoon. The first thing Marshal Garrick Ruhl did when he stepped out of the coach and saw him was draw his six-gun.

"You're under arrest." At the surprise on Todd's face, the marshal added, "I just came from Denver. I learned all about you. Your name ain't Douglas Brock. Your name is Todd Kildow and you're wanted for murder."

It sounded feeble and lame and Todd knew the marshal wouldn't believe him, but he told about coming to give himself up.

"Sure, you was," the marshal said. "Now march." He had a six-gun in his hand and Todd's Remington stuck in his belt.

"March? Where?" Todd asked. A dozen townsmen watched, curious.

"We ain't got a jail, but there's a stout cabin on Front Street where I can hold a feller till the next stage. March."

Todd walked, following the marshal's directions.

The marshal's six-gun was never more than a foot away from his spine. Townsmen followed, asking questions.

"What's he done, Mr. Ruhl?"

"He's wanted in Kansas for a double murder. Shot two men from ambush. Didn't give them a chance."

"He's a killer," someone said. "Shot old Hank over at the Gold Palace last night. Shot right through a door and put three slugs in 'im."

The cabin on Front Street was almost exactly like Marietta Manahan's: one room, one door and one window. It was built of heavy timbers, and the one window was boarded over from the outside.

"What you gonna do with 'im, marshal? Hang 'im?"

"No. I'm taking him back to Kansas. I'll have to stand guard here all night, I reckon, unless somebody volunteers."

"It's a long ways to Kansas. Best hang 'im here. We ain't never had a hangin' in White River. It'd be a way of discouragin' some of these robbers around here."

"No. My duty is to turn him over to the sheriff in Kansas."

"Too bad. We ain't never had a hangin'."

The cabin was empty. Not even a cot. Todd stood in the center of the room and tried to reason with the marshal. "I know you won't believe me, but I really did plan to give myself up. Believe it or not, I know who the third man is, one of the three who murdered my folks. He's here in White River."

"Yeah, I know about your folks being murdered. The marshal in Denver's got a letter from Sheriff Hocker telling all about it. But the fact is you're a wanted man."

"Do you know J.D. Hays? I mean, do you know

very much about him?"

"I know him."

"I believe he was the one that got away in the dark that night in Kansas."

"Can you prove that?"

"Maybe he'll admit it. He's already told some folks he came through western Kansas and lost two partners in an ambush. He came through Kansas at the same time my folks were murderd."

"You think he'll admit it?"

"Ask him. You're a lawman and you know how to ask questions."

Three townsmen had followed them into the cabin, and they looked first at Todd and then at the marshal.

Marshal Ruhl fixed a stern glare on Todd. "Tell me something, son. Do you really think he'd admit murder? You've got to have some proof."

Todd's shoulders slumped. Suddenly his legs were weak, and he was very tired. All he could do was shake his head.

"Maybe it's my duty to at least ask him," the marshal said. "I'll go see him and put it to him as soon as I can get somebody to relieve me here. Without a lockup, somebody'll have to stand guard. Now, empty your pockets and take off your boots."

Todd did as ordered. His folding knife was taken and his boots and pant legs were searched for a hideout gun. He was allowed to put his boots back on. His hands were tied behind his back. For a second, when the marshal holstered his six-gun and took a short piece of rope from one of the townsmen, he had a chance. He weighed it in his mind and ruled it out. It was only a small chance, and he was too tired to run. Too damned tired of hiding from the law. When everyone left and the door was latched from

207

the outside, he sat on the splintery wooden floor.

At dusk, the marshal brought him a sandwich and a jug of water, untied his hands until he ate and drank, then re-tied them. When the marshal left, Todd heard men's voices outside, and he knew from the conversation that a volunteer was guarding the door. With the darkness came an even darker mood. It was hopeless. There was no way in the world to get J.D. Hays to confess to anything.

And when he was honest with himself he wasn't even absolutely sure that Hays was the man. Hell, he couldn't identify him, and Hays coming through Kansas and losing two partners in an ambush could have been just a coincidence. His partners could have died in a fight with Indians like he said.

Everything was hopeless.

He sat with his back against a wall. Twisting his wrists was painful, but he discovered he could at least twist them. His fingers groped at the knot in the rope, but he couldn't untie it. Straining, he tried, then gave up.

What the hell was the use?

He was half asleep when he first heard the tapping. At first he thought he was imagining it, but there it was again.

And suddenly his nerves came alert, taut.

It was coming from the window. Somebody was tapping on the boards that covered the window. Moving quietly, Todd go to his feet and made his way in the dark to that end of the cabin. The tapping sounded again. He put his ear to the window boards.

Heard his name whispered, "Todd?" A woman's whisper.

CHAPTER TWENTY-THREE

"Marrie," Todd said in a hushed tone. "Marrie, get away from there."

"Shhh. There's a man near the front door."

He whispered, "Marrie, don't do anything foolish. I'm tied up and can't get away."

"I've got a long knife, Todd. I'm going to pry one of these boards loose."

"Don't, Marrie. Don't get yourself in trouble."

A nail creaked. Creaked again.

"Damnit, Marrie, will you get away from there!"

"Shhh." A board creaked. He could hear her prying with the knife, prying on a board. A loosening nail screeched like a prairie owl, or so it seemed to Todd.

He groaned inwardly. She was going to get caught and she was going to be in serious trouble. The nail screeched again.

"Here, Todd. Take this. It's a knife. I think I can squeeze it through."

"I can't. My hands are tied. Get away from there, will you."

"Then, goshdamn it, take it in your teeth."

He put his face against the window boards and moved slowly, groping with his right cheek. One of the boards was no longer nailed tight, and he could feel a slight breeze. Then his nose came into contact with a wooden knife handle. He opened his mouth and got hold of it. He pulled back. The knife came through.

"Got it?"

With the knife in his mouth he couldn't answer. He squatted, bent low and placed the knife on the floor. Standing, he whispered, "Yeah. Now what?"

"Cut yourself loose and I'll hand you a gun."

"Marrie, this is dumb. It's all for nothing."

"No it isn't. Just do it, goshdamn it."

Cut himself loose. Sure. How?

Sitting, he groped with his hands behind his back until he found the knife. It was a long one, a butcher knife. He twisted his wrists and tried to cut the rope that bound them, but all he did was cut himself. There had to be a way.

He shifted positions and was on his knees. By feel, he got the knife handle between his boots with the blade pointing up. If he sat back, he thought grimly, he'd puncture himself right where he sat. All right, try to cut the rope.

"Are you free, Todd?"

Now he was the one who whispered, "Shhh."

The knife came loose and fell over. He groped with his hands and got it back in position. Tried to hold it tight between his boots. There. Now. He felt the rope come into contact with the knife blade. He moved his wrists up and down.

Damn.

The knife fell over again.

Try. Try like a steer. If he could get it between the shanks of his boots he might be able to hold it. There. Try again. He cut his left hand. Moved his wrists up and down. Felt one strand of the rope part. Kept working at it. Another strand parted. Then the knife fell over.

Do it again. Got it. Now.

The third strand parted and he was free.

Rubbing his wrists, he stood slowly and listened. The man outside the door coughed and spat.

With his mouth against the window boards, Todd whispered, "Marrie. I'm loose."

"Here."

The board creeked again.

"Shhh. Quiet."

"I can't get this gun through. I have to . . ." Her voice was strained. The board creaked. "I think it'll go now. Here."

"I've got it. Now get out of here."

"My horse is saddled and tied behind this cabin, Todd. Go to my cabin in the woods. I'll be there in the morning as soon as I can get another horse. Will you do that?"

"Yeah. Now git."

"See you, partner."

The gun was a long-barreled one. He guessed from the feel of it that it was one of the old converted cap-and-ball pistols. His groping fingers told him it was loaded with metallic cartridges. It might misfire, but it didn't matter. He didn't want to shoot anyone anyway. Just threaten the guard.

How? Had to get him inside.

Hell, when the idea came to him it was simple. He put his mouth to the window boards again. "Marrie. Are you there, Marrie?" No answer. She was gone. Good.

He pushed on the loose board. It squeeked and creaked. Pushed again until it fell onto the ground outside. That let the night air in, but the hole in the window wasn't big enough to crawl through, and he knew he couldn't pry another board off without alerting the guard outside. All right, he'd try something else. He kicked the wall, stomped the floor, then hurried to the door.

The outside door latch was slid open. Door hinges creaked. A lantern appeared in the door with a man behind it. Todd flattened himself against the wall next to the door. The lantern came through. It illuminated the window and the gaping hole in it.

"Shit," a man muttered. The lantern bobbed toward the window with the man following it.

Moving fast, Todd poked the long-barrel of the pistol into the man's back. "Hold it."

"Wha . . ."

"This is a gun in your back. Just stand right there. Don't move a hair."

"What? How?"

Todd's groping fingers found the man's right arm and the gun at the end of it. He twisted the weapon free. "I don't mean you any harm, mister, but I aim to get out of here. Just stand right there and be quiet."

"How'd you get loose? Where'd you get the gun?"

Another idea popped into Todd's mind, and he chuckled a dry chuckle. "The only gun I've got is yours. You just plain got fooled, mister. Now get up against that wall."

The guard did as he was told. Todd picked up the knife. Now there was no evidence that he'd had any help at all. They would wonder how he'd got his hands untied and what he'd poked into the guard's back, but they'd never know.

Outside, Todd slammed the door and shot the bolt. A half-moon cast a dim glow over the town of White River, and tall pines threw long black shadows across the outlines of cabins. Somewhere, a dog barked. Windows in two cabins down the street were lit up. Todd threw the knife into a clump of aspens across the street, and made his way to the rear of the jail-cabin.

He heard the horse before he saw it. The horse stamped its feet and snorted at the sight of a man approaching, and then Todd saw it tied to a lodgepole pine. "Whoa, boy. Whoa, now." He put the guard's six-gun in the empty holster on his right hip and stuck the long-barreled pistol under his belt. "Whoa, feller."

A whisper came from the dark, "Todd, is that you?"

He couldn't see her. "Yeah." He saw her when she stepped away from the shadow of a ponderosa. "Go back to your place, Marrie. Lock the door."

"I will. I'll see you tomorrow, Todd. All right? I will, won't I?"

"Yeah." He gathered the reins and stepped into the saddle. "Marrie?"

"Yes?"

"Thanks."

"Adios, partner."

He rode at a trot toward the river. When he crossed the far end of Main Street, he could see lights from the Gold Palace. The horse stepped into the dark water without hesitation and splashed across. Black shadows made the wagon road invisible to Todd, but the horse could see and knew where it was going. "That-a-boy," Todd said quietly. "You find the way."

A quarter mile farther Todd reined up suddenly. Something didn't sound right. He listened. Yeah, it was another horse crossing the river behind him. Either it was a sourdough heading back to his diggings or somebody was following him. He had an urge to get into the woods and wait and see who it was. But it was too dark to see. All he could do was to go on.

"Walk with soft steps, feller, but let's go." The

horse moved out readily. Todd could barely make out the animal's head and neck. The saddle swayed, dipped, tilted and rocked. They crossed the first creek, and eventually came to the second one. Without being told what to do, the horse turned north.

There it was again. Todd listened. Somebody or something was behind him. Listened carefully. Whatever it was, it stopped too, then turned and went back toward town. Somebody had followed him this far but no farther.

Damn. that presented a problem. Did whoever it was figure out where Todd was going? How many people knew about Marrie's mountain cabin? Hell. But when he thought it over he knew he had to go on. That was where Marrie expected to find him. He'd go on.

When he rode through the willows, the branches almost dragged him from the saddle. He put his head down and hung onto the saddlehorn. His broad-brimmed hat protected his face.

They crossed the creek again and Todd kept his hold on the saddlehorn, knowing they were heading into the timber. The saddle swayed and dipped. His knees were cramped from riding stirrups too short for him and he took his feet out of the stirrups and let them hang down.

Finally, they broke out of the timber and crossed the creek again, and he could see the cabin in the middle of the moonlit meadow.

Approaching with caution, he stopped fifty feet away and listened, He rode around the cabin. There was no horse and no sign of life. He tied his horse to a hitching post in front of the cabin, and walked to the door. Again, he listened. Breathing in shallow breaths, he pushed on the door and stepped back.

The door creaked open. There was no other sound. Todd fumbled a sulphur match out of a shirt pocket with his left hand, struck it with a thumbnail and stepped inside. A six-gun was in his right hand. The coal-oil lamp was still there in the middle of the table. He went to it, dropped the match when it burned his fingers, struck another and lit the lamp.

He was alone, but he knew someone had been there. Two of the airtight cans of grub Marrie had left behind had been opened, emptied and tossed on the floor. A side of venison hung on a short rope from a ceiling rafter.

Quickly, he blew out the lamp and went to the horse. Instead of mounting, he led the horse back the way they had come until they were at the creek. There he found a tree limb to tie the horse to, and loosened the cinches. "Sorry I can't turn you loose to graze, feller, but I might need you in a hurry."

Nothing to do but wait for daylight. Sit on the ground and wait. He shivered and hugged his knees. "Seems like this's all I do," he muttered. While he sat there, he tried to figure out what to do when daylight came. He'd promised the girl he'd meet her here. What then? They'd talked about grabbing J.D. Hays somehow and forcing a confession out of him, but that was foolish. How could they grab him? Where would they take him? How could they get the deputy U.S. marshal to witness the confession?

And the big question: Was J.D. Hays the man?

Lying on his side with his knees drawn up and his hat for a pillow, he dozed fitfully. Once, he got up and stamped his feet and waved his arms to get the blood circulating. He lay down and dozed off again.

When he woke up he found himself looking into the face of a grinning savage.

CHAPTER TWENTY-FOUR

"Huh," Todd snorted, jerking upright. His hand went to the stolen six-gun, but he didn't draw it. "Where the smokey hell did you come from?"

The Indian squatted on his heels twenty feet away, grinning. He carried a colt six-shooter in a holster on his left hip, butt forward. His leather britches were dirty and worn, and he still wore the white man's muslin shirt under the black vest.

For a moment, the Indian just grinned, then he raised his right hand shoulder high, put his index and middle fingers together and raised his hand higher.

"Friend, huh?" Todd stood sorely. He could feel his knees pop. "Well, I'm sure as hell glad you're not an enemy. How the hell do you do that? Sneak up on a man that way? And what're you doing around here?"

No answer. Instead, the Indian held out a hand with the index finger pointing up. He quickly brought the hand toward himself.

"Go with you? Where?"

Standing and still grinning, the young savage made the same sign and walked away toward the cabin. Todd untied the dun horse and followed, leading the horse. The cabin door was open, and the red man walked right in. Todd tied the horse to the hitching post and went in behind him. A fire was going in the cookstove, and without a sound, the Indian sliced two filets from the side of venison, opened the stove and put them in the fire.

"Breakfast, huh? Well, anything's better than nothing." Todd sat on the cot and put his elbows on his knees. The Indian squatted on the floor next to the door. After a while he stood and jerked his left fist down from the waist.

"Yeah, I'll wait," Todd said. "I've got nowhere to go anyhow."

Todd watched through the door as the red man walked around the cabin, studied the timber surrounding the grassy meadow, the sky, the ground, the trees again. He stepped aside as the Indian came back and lifted the lid off the stove. Flames were wrapped around the meat.

Todd wondered where the Indian's horses were, but he didn't know how to ask. He knew the Indian had two horses now.

When the meat was cooked, black on the outside, it was lifted out of the stove with a long, pointed willow stick. The savage picked up a piece, dropped it on the stove, picked it up again, handling it carefully to keep from burning his fingers, and blew the ashes off it. He took a bite, chewed, and motioned for Todd to do the same.

"Hell of a way to cook," Todd muttered, but he did as the Indian had done. The meat needed salt, but wasn't bad. It was grub and it would stick to a man's ribs.

Their meal over, Todd watched as his new-found friend again walked outside, walked easily like a man taking a morning stroll, came back.

But inside, the savage quickly slammed the door

and waved his hand wildly.

"What? What's the matter?"

With a hand pointing up under his chin, the Indian nodded.

"A man? There's a man out there? How many?" Todd held a hand shoulder high, palm up, and wagged his hand right to left.

The Indian held up four fingers.

"Four of them, huh? They must have guessed where I was headed and they've come to take me back. Damn." He hurried to the window and looked out. He saw no sign of life. Opening the door a crack, he scanned the woods in front of the cabin. Still nothing. "Are you sure? I don't see anything."

No answer was needed. A bullet drilled a hole in the plank floor and a split-second later a rifle cracked.

"Damn. You're right. They mean to take me back dead or alive and they just as soon take me dead." He drew the stolen six-gun and went to the window. Another bullet poked through the burlap bag that covered the window and thudded into the bar wall.

The red man opened the door, dropped onto his stomach in front of it, aimed his pistol and fired.

Todd glanced his way, then looked out the window again. Now he saw movement back in the trees. He fired at it, but knew he hadn't hit anything. "No use wasting ammunition," he muttered. "They're too far away for short guns." Another bullet zipped through the window, past Todd's head, and shattered the lamp globe on the table. "But," he said through clenched teeth, "not too far away for a rifle."

Another lead slug hit the far wall, and still another dug a splintery furrow in the floor three inches from the Indian's right shoulder. The Indian rolled over—

out of the doorway—got to his knees and looked around the edge of the doorjamb.

Stepping away from the window, Todd said matter-of-factly, "We're in a hell of a spot, ain't we? We're in the middle of a meadow and they're back in the trees. They can shoot at us all day, and if we try to run for it they can pick us off before we get twenty feet."

Only a grunt came from the Indian.

Looking out the window again, Todd talked on. "You picked the wrong white man to make friends with." He took a longer look. "Well, maybe we can hold them off 'til night and slip away in the dark."

But he knew night would be a long time coming.

Ten minutes passed before more shots were fired. One sang an angry song through the window and another zinged into the floor near the door. The two men inside didn't return the fire. They both knew they had to conserve their ammunition in case of an all-out attack. More time passed. The sun was halfway to its peak. Only an occasional shot came from the trees. The riflemen had to let them know they were still there. What did they plan to do? Get more guns from town and then rush the cabin? Sneak up on the blind side and set the cabin afire?

Probably waiting for more guns.

The Indian kept his position on the floor, taking a quick look every few seconds. Todd did the same at the window.

"Hey," Todd said, "what's your name?"

He got only a blank stare.

Todd pointed at himself and said, "Todd." He

pointed at the Indian and said, "What's your name?" Still only a blank stare. "Seems like if we're gonna fight side-by-side and maybe die we ought to know each other's names."

No response.

"I have to call you something. How about, uh . . ."

The Indian flipped open the loading gate of his Colt revolver and counted the bullets.

"How about Pistol? That's a good name." He pointed at himself and said, "Todd." He pointed at his red-skinned friend and said, "Pistol."

Another lead slug tore into the floor near the door. Pistol didn't even blink.

"Well, I'll tell you, Pistol, as soon as they get more help, they're gonna shoot us out of here. Won't be long. Hell's gonna open up."

White clouds gathered in the west, and by noon they'd turned dark. Shortly after noon, they obliterated the sun. Todd muttered to himself, "Gonna rain, but what difference does it make? Any minute now the air is gonna be full of lead."

Pistol paid him no mind, but kept glancing out the door from his position on the floor.

And then the shooting began.

Four rifle shots split the quiet, one right after the other. Todd instinctively ducked below the window. The shots didn't come through the window. He glanced at the Indian. They hadn't come through the door either. Four more shots, rapid-fire.

Feeling like a target with a bullseye painted on his face, Todd rose up and looked out. Two more shots. Rifle shots. They were coming from the woods across the meadow. Either they were surrounded or that was somebody else over there. Somebody with a repeating rifle. And then it came to him.

Marrie.

"Hey, Pistol, we've got an ally. Look." He pointed to the far side of the meadow. The Indian was already looking, puzzled. "A friend, " Todd said. "Hey." When Pistol looked his way, he held his left hand shoulder high, extended two fingers and raised his hand higher. "A friend."

Nodding, the Indian indicated he understood.

"Let's give her a chance to reload and then run like hell."

A long minute passed, and another shot came from over there. "All right friend, let's go." Todd went to the door, motioned for the Indian to follow and ran.

A bullet whistled past his ear, then four rapid shots came from the other direction. Todd ran to the horse, untied it and ran for the woods, leading the horse. The Indian was right behind him. The shooting continued, nearly all of it coming from ahead. The dun horse led easily, trotting behind Todd. The Indian was beside the horse. There was more shooting.

He could see her now, against a tree on one knee, in her baggy overalls, aiming and shooting as fast as she could lever cartridges into the firing chamber. The men behind him fired twice, but their shots went wild. They didn't have time to take aim. Marrie's bullets were keeping them down.

She yelled at him, "Hurry, Todd. I have to reload."

He hurried, and then he was at her side. He let go of the horse and it went on a way, stepped on a rein and stopped. The Indian hit the ground beside them.

Winded from the run, Todd gasped, "Marrie, you're an angel. You're an angel with a gun."

She was reloading, taking shells one at a time from a pocket of her overalls and shoving them into the side of the Winchester. The ground around her was littered with empty shell casings.

A poke in the ribs got Todd's attention. The Indian was crawling backward and motioning for them to follow. "Yeah, we've got to git," Todd said. "They'll get more help pretty soon and they'll be all around us."

She said, "Right," and started crawling backward too, hanging onto the rifle. A few strands of red hair hung below her floppy hat.

They crawled until they were deeper into the timber, out of sight of the meadow, then stood and ran, following the Indian, Todd leading the dun horse.

"I don't . . . know where he's going," Todd puffed, "but he . . . seems to know."

"I know," she said.

They ran five hundred yards, until Todd's legs were threatening to buckle, and came to the edge of a narrow, grassy draw. Three horses were down there, one saddled and two hobbled.

"The hobbled horses are his," she gasped, "and the saddled one is a livery horse I rented."

No more words were spoken as the Indian unwrapped his homemade hobbles and swung up onto one of the horses. Marrie mounted her horse and Todd got on the dun. As they rode out of the draw, Todd saw two saddles on the ground beside the reins of a campfire. The Indian kept going, riding bareback and handling his horse with nothing more than a rope in its mouth. They followed.

For two miles they rode at a lope, dodging tree limbs. The horses jumped over downed timbers and dodged boulders. Marrie hung onto her rifle and rode easily, as comfortable as if she were in a rocking chair. They rode along the edge of a canyon and then around the end of it and to the other side. There the red man reined up and slid off his horse. The horses were blowing hard from the run. Todd and the girl stayed on horseback and watched the Indian walk, bent low to the rim of the canyon. When he returned he motioned for them to dismount.

"He can see a long ways from here," Todd commented. "If anyone is after us, we'll be mounted again and long gone before they can get around this big hole in the ground."

"Yeah, but how do we get back to town? Or are we going to keep going?"

"I don't know. Let's see what he does."

What the red man did was sit cross-legged on the ground. They followed suit. For a moment, no one spoke. Todd broke the silence.

"I'm guessing, Marrie, that you came to meet me, heard gunfire, saw the men and got around to the other side."

"Right. I fired a lot of shots. I hope I didn't hit anyone. I only wanted to keep them from shooting at you."

"You did exactly the right thing." Todd grinned. "Boy, if I ever get in another gun battle, I wanta keep you and your long gun on my side."

A grunt from the Indian brought their attention to him. His black eyes were somber as he held his right hand next to his heart and then swept it to the ground, palm up. He repeated it. Todd nodded.

"What is he saying?"

"He says his heart is on the ground. He's sad about something."

Watching their faces, the Indian moved his hands again. This time he touched the right side of his chest with a clenched fist. Again.

Todd nodded in understanding. "Father."

Next, the savage pointed at his lips with two fingers and slowly moved his hand away.

224

"Brother. His dad and brother."

Silently, they watched the Indian hold his hands shoulder high as if he were shooting a rifle.

"Uh-oh." Todd said. "I think he's saying they were shot."

Marietta Manahan gasped when the red man opened his shirt and showed them the ugly scar along his right side. "Is he saying he was shot too?"

"Looks like it."

A dark finger drawn across the Indian's brow told Todd something else.

"A white man."

Three fingers were held up.

"Three white men."

All were silent as the message became clear, and suddenly Todd grunted, "Good God a-mighty."

"What, Todd?"

"Three white men shot him and his dad and brother. I first saw him in eastern Colorado Territory. He could have come from Kansas. He once told me he was hunting. You don't . . . it couldn't be . . ." Todd's voice dropped off as the thought sunk in.

Marrie was excited. "Todd, is he saying his dad and brother were murdered by the same three men who murdered your folks? And is he hunting them too?"

CHAPTER TWENTY-FIVE

Todd turned it over in his mind. "It could be. Damn, I wish we could talk to him with words. Hmm. I'm gonna try something." He signaled a question, then made a V of his fingers under his right eye and looked along the fingers. He made the question sign again. The Indian nodded. Now he made the sign for white man, held up three fingers, and made the sign for hunting again. Another nod.

"He's hunting them," Todd said. "Now, here comes the hard part." He tried to remember the sign for mother, couldn't, so he curled the fingers of his right hand and made a motion as if combing his hair. A nod. What next? He pointed at himself. That brought a quizzical look.

"What's the matter, Todd?"

"I made the sign for woman, and he wonders if I meant my woman." He shook his head negatively and tried again. This time he signaled father and woman, then brought his fist down from in front of his neck as if he was holding something. That got the reaction he wanted, another nod.

"We're getting it," Todd said, excitement in his voice. He went through the same motions the Indian had gone through to indicate shoot, held up three fingers and drew one finger across his forehead. He couldn't remember the sign for death.

Marietta Manahan was getting more excited by the minute. "What you're saying is three white men shot your father and mother. And I think he understands."

The Indian was nodding, a grim expression on his dark face.

"Yeah, I think he understands. So far, anyhow. But I'm not through." Todd pointed at himself, and made the V sign with his fingers, then held up one finger. That got a puzzled expression.

"Aw, I did that wrong. How can I tell him? I'll try this." Pointing at himself, he next indicated shoot, held up two fingers, and indicated white men.

That got a reaction. The Indian made the sign for question, pointed at Todd, made the sign for shoot and then two white men. Todd nodded affirmatively.

"Hey, we're getting down to it now. I think he knows I shot two of them. Let's see." Todd made the V sign for hunt, held up one finger, then drew the finger across his forehead to indicate a white man's hat. The Indian went through the same signals and nodded.

"What does that mean, Todd?"

"I'm not sure. Either he's telling me he understands or he's telling me he's hunting one white man too."

"That's what I was thinking. We have to find out."

A grunt, and the red man went through the same motions, paused, then held his right hand shoulder high with the fingers curled upward. He slowly brought the hand toward his chest.

"What? Damn, I don't understand."

Again, the Indian went through the hunt-one-white-man motions, then pretended to pick up something with his thumb and forefinger.

228

"Huh?" Todd's mouth dropped open.

"What is it, Todd, what is it?"

In a voice strained with excitement, Todd answered, "I think he said he found him. Yeah, that's what he said. He said he is looking for one white man and then he said he found him. Or found something."

"Where?"

"I don't know. I don't know how to ask."

He didn't have to. The red man went through the same signals he'd gone through before: one hand up, fingers curved, and the hand drawn toward him.

"Near," Todd gasped. "He's somewhere near."

"It makes sense, Todd. Why is he staying around these parts? And why was he prowling down alleys? He's been looking for a man and he's found him."

"Yeah. Damn. You're right. And the three men who shot his dad and brother, I'll bet he got a look at them. They thought he was dead, and he might have played dead, but I'll bet he knows that man when he sees him."

"All right." Marrie was squirming with excitement. "You both are looking for the same man, and he knows where the man is. But . . ." Suddenly her shoulders slumped. "If that's so, why hasn't he killed the man? That's what he wants to do, isn't it?"

"Yeah, he wants him dead, but he wants more than that. He wants a scalp. He can't just shoot him from a distance, he has to get his hands on him."

"And if he does," Marrie added, "he'll kill him."

"Yeah." Todd was glum now. "And I'll be right back where I started."

"Hmm. Yes. Unless we find that gentleman first."

"Uh-huh. We think we know who he is, but we're not sure."

"I wish there was a way to point J.D. Hays out to

our red-skinned friend here."

"Yeah. But I can't think of a way. Can you?"

A long pause, then, "No. Unless . . . Sometimes, old Hays pays a visit to one of the, uh, whorehouses. Talk has it he's got a favorite whore and sometimes he goes over there late at night before he goes to bed."

"You'd think he'd have all the women he wanted."

"Yes, but talk has it he's kind of . . . he likes something unnatural, and he's got a favorite whore someplace."

"Do you happen to know where?"

"No. I've seen him slip out the back door and I asked where he was going, and all I heard was he was going to his favorite whorehouse."

"He goes out the back door, you say?"

"Yes. He always took Hank with him. Hmm. I wonder if he'll go alone."

"I'd give anything to know where he goes. Or, hell, I'd give anything to know when he goes. Always late at night, you say?"

"I've only seen him go twice, and both times it was around two o'clock."

"The back door?"

"Yes. As if he didn't want anyone to know."

The Indian was listening and watching without expression.

"What I have to do, then," Todd said, "is wait somewhere near the back door and see if he comes out."

"And then?"

"And then put a gun at his head and march him someplace in the light. And then I have to get Pistol here to take a look at him."

"Pistol."

"Our Cheyenne friend. That's not his name, but I had to call him something."

230

"Oh. Hmm. There's only one place I can think of, Todd, and that's my place. My cabin."

"Naw. Not there. You could be in trouble already. If those gents back there got a look at you, you're in trouble, and I don't want you to get in so far you can't get out."

"They didn't see me, and they don't know I helped you get away from that cabin of a jail."

"Then you'd be a fool to take any more chances."

"Nobody ever accused me of being very bright. I've done foolish things before."

"We'll meet someplace else. All we need is a lantern. And old Hays."

"And some luck."

"Yeah. Now . . ." Todd got to his knees and crawled to the edge of the canyon, took a good long look and crawled back. "We've got to get back to town, but we'd better wait for dark."

"And we've got to take him with us."

A glance at the sky told Todd it would be dark in about two hours. It also told him rain was coming. "Let's get on horseback and take our time, try to get to town just after dark."

She stood and went to her horse. "There's another way back, but I'm not sure I know the trails."

"If we can get across the river we can come into town from another direction. There's got to be another place where we can ride across."

"Let's head for the river and find one."

Looking at the Indian, Todd held out his right hand with the index finger pointing up. He quickly brought the hand toward himself. The Indian nodded and stood.

"I wish I knew how to say 'town' in sign language. I wish I knew how to say a lot of things."

"He seems to understand. He's going to his horse."

When they were mounted, Todd took the lead, heading in the direction he believed the river to be. The dun horse was tiring, and Todd was sympathetic. "You've had this saddle on your back a long time, old feller. There are better days ahead, I'll guarantee."

After a few miles, the Indian rode abreast of Todd and made the signal to follow, then went ahead. He turned east between two high piney hills, then went south along the spine of a boulder-strewn ridge. A couple of miles farther, he reined his horse down off the ridge and followed a creek. The clouds had covered the sky now, and lightning zig-zagged to the west. Thunder cracked as if the earth had split open.

Nobody spoke as a cold rain began to fall. Within minutes everyone was wet and cold. The Indian rode on, following the creek, and after three more miles they came to the river.

Lightning hit a granite boulder behind them. A clap of thunder followed, and echoed among the ridge. Static electricity pulled on their hair. The river was swift here and belly deep to a horse. The bottom was covered with hat-sized rocks. A man on foot would have been knocked off his feet by the rushing water. Todd kicked his boots out of the stirrups and was ready to throw himself clear if the horse stumbled over the rocks and went down. The girl did the same. The Indian, riding bareback, showed no concern at all. The horses waded across and scrambled up onto the far bank.

From there they went east over a ridge, down and across a valley, through heavy timber and then up a rocky, brush-covered hill. Riding bareback, the Indian had to hang on to his horse's mane going up the hills. The rain had slowed to a sprinkle, but it was a cold sprinkle. Near the top of the hill the Indian reined up and slid down. He looked at Todd and the girl and jerked his right fist downward twice.

"He wants to stay here," Todd said. "The town must be over that hill."

The girl dismounted and hugged herself. "I feel like a drowned rat."

"You know, Marrie, you don't have to wait here. You can go on back to your cabin and build a fire and get warm. I'll stay here 'til after dark."

"I'm staying." With that, she sat on a small boulder, pulled her knees up and wrapped her arms around them.

The red man squatted on the ground. Todd stood.

"I wish we could talk to him verbally," she said. "I'm just bursting with curiosity about him."

"I am too. I can make a guess about him, but it's only a guess."

"What would you guess?"

"I'm guessing he and his dad and brother were camping somewhere alone, probably hunting, and three white men came up on them and opened fire. The Indians were shot down, and the white men . . . Oh." Todd stopped in mid-sentence, suddenly remembering something. He pointed at the skinning knife in a decorated sheath fastened to the Indian's belt. "I took that off one of the men I shot. When Pistol there saw it I thought his eyes were gonna pop out of his head. I'll bet that knife belonged to him or his dad or brother."

"Really? If that's so then it's certain that you two are after the same man."

"I'll bet it's so. The white men thought the three Cheyennes were dead and they took what little of value the Indians had and left. Pistol there was shot and hurt bad, but somehow he lived. It took him a long time to get well, maybe a year, and he went

233

looking for the three white men.''

"But he'd gotten a good look at them. He could recognize them.''

"Uh-huh. Lucky for me, or he'd think I was one of them, what with me having the knife. But he couldn't just ride into a town and ask questions like I did. He had to sneak around in the dark.''

"He has a lot of perseverance. Both of you do.''

"I wonder . . . I wonder if he knows that two of the killers are dead. I wish I knew the sign language for death.''

"You tried to tell him, and I'll bet he does know. As a matter of fact, I've got a suspicion he understands more of what we're saying than we realize.''

"I hope so. I wish I could talk Cheyenne.''

Their conversation was ignored by the Indian. The sky to the west was clearing and the rain had stopped. But the sun had gone down behind a faraway ridge, and the air was cold. The white man and woman shivered in the cold. The Indian showed no discomfort at all.

Finally, it was dark.

"We can go now,'' the girl said, standing. "We can all go to my cabin and get dry and warm.''

"We'll have to be careful and stay away from lights, but unless somebody suspects you of helping me, I think we'll all be safe in your cabin.''

"Then let's go before we catch pneumonia.'' She want to her horse.

Todd got the Indian's attention and gave the signal for "come.'' He gathered the reins and mounted the dun horse. The red man followed suit. They were quiet as the horses picked their way to the top of the hill. From there they could see dim lantern lights from the town below. Again, they let the horses find the way. Marietta Manahan's rented horse knew where the livery barn was and was eager to get there. The other horses followed. In places the hill was so steep the horses slid, and in other places they had to go around boulders and gulleys that the humans couldn't see.

They were on the outskirts of town now, and the girl had to argue with the stable horse to keep it from going directly to the livery barn. The streets were soaked from the rain but too rocky to be muddy. Then they were behind her cabin.

"We can put the horses inside the fence," she whispered. "Why don't you wait here while I go inside and light a lamp. I'll put a blanket or something over the window."

"All right. We'll wait 'til you get a lamp lit." Todd tried to see the Indian in the dark. Couldn't. "Hey, Pistol." No answer. "Hey, speak, grunt, say something." And then he knew.

"He's gone, Marrie. He just took off in the dark."

"He couldn't have. I can see his horse."

"But he's not on it."

"Well . . . what's he up to? Where is he going without a horse?"

"I don't know," Todd whispered. "But I'm betting he's got a plan."

CHAPTER TWENTY-SIX

Marietta Manahan had some wood chopped and stored in a box beside the stove, and it didn't take long to get a fire going. They both stood in front of the open oven door, soaking warmth.

"Turn your head, Todd."

"Why?"

"I've got to get out of these wet clothes."

"Oh." He faced the window and held his hands over the stove, warming them. Gradually the chill left his body. Clothes rustled behind him, and now that he was warm, he couldn't help remembering how she'd looked with that red dress down to her waist. What would she do if he just turned around? It would be her own fault, wouldn't it? After all, she knew he was a man, and man couldn't stay in a one-room cabin with a pretty naked girl without feeling a powerful urge. What would she do? What would happen?

"You can turn around now."

Too late.

She was wearing overalls again and a plaid shirt. They were clean and dry. A pair of boys' socks covered her feet. Her sorrel hair was still wet and stringy, and she grabbed a towel and rubbed it dry.

"You ought to get out of your clothes, too, Todd,

and wrap a blanket around yourself while your clothes dry." Her hair was puffed up now, like a big fuzzy ball.

"Me? Stand here with nothing on but a blanket?"

"Why not? We're adults."

"Yeah, that's the trouble."

"Oh." One side of her mouth turned up. "I see. You think then that despite all that's happened in the past twenty-four hours and all that's going to happen, we should make love?"

"That idea did come to my head, yeah."

Her smile widened. "Know something? That idea came into my head too." The smile dropped. "But I shoved it away. I'm no virgin, I think I told you that, but the next time I go to bed with a man he'll be my man for keeps. And I'll be his woman. No more experimenting."

"Yeah." He looked away from her.

"Besides, we've got other things to do."

"Yeah."

"Like some supper?"

"Uh-huh." He had to do some shoving too. He shoved away the mental image of her in the red dress. "Did you say old Hays goes to his favorite . . . whore about two o'clock?"

"Right around that time. You might have a long wait in the alley. He might not even come out."

"That looks like my only chance to get him alone."

"You'll have to try. Meanwhile, I'll put the skillet on. We've got time to kill."

While she washed the supper dishes he wiped them with a flour sack that had been ripped apart at the seams and made into a towel. They sat at the table and drank the rest of the coffee. He wanted to get moving, but it was too early.

"Tell me more about yourself, Todd."

"I've told you just about everything. What about you?"

"Well, as my sister told you, we were raised on a ranch, what cowboys call a big outfit. My dad keeps a wagon out for at least two months in the spring when they gather calves, and again for a month or so in the fall when they gather beef. My dad is rich and powerful. He has always been active in Republican politics. Quite a few men got elected to public office with his help. Now, Leslie tells me he is going to run for the U.S. Senate. He'll win. He has plenty of politicians who owe him and who know how to get votes."

"And you," Todd put in, "you're the rebel. The red-haired daughter of a rich rancher who has a mind of her own. A girl who likes a challenge and likes to do things most women wouldn't think of."

Her mouth turned up slightly. "You're mostly right. Only some of the things I've done were things most women do think of. The difference is they only think about it."

"What will you do when this is over? When I'm either a free man or a convicted killer?"

"I'm going to do something for the rights of women. I don't know exactly what, but something." She was pensive for a moment. "Oh, I don't mean I'll make that my life's goal and forsake home and family, but whatever I can do I'll do."

"The last thing you want to do then is go home and live on the ranch and be a ranch wife." He tried to disguise the question as idle talk, but he found himself breathing shallowly as he waited for her answer.

She answered quickly, "Oh no, I wouldn't rule that out. Like I said, I believe in rights for women and want to do something about it, but a certain kind of man could keep me from being a plumb radical."

"What kind of a man would it take, Marrie?" Now his pulse was racing, and he swallowed hard. What's the matter with me, he asked himself.

"Do you really want to know or are you just making conversation?"

"I'd like to know." He was nervous. "I've never met anybody like you. I'll always wonder what became of you, no matter what happens."

The half-smile gave her green eyes an impish glint. "You don't have to wonder."

"Huh?"

"You asked what kind of man it would take. Do you really, really want to know?"

"Yes." Here it comes.

"Your kind."

All he could do was stare at her. She stared right back.

Then, "Surprised, Todd?"

"Surprised?" He exhaled and grinned a weak grin. "I reckon."

"Pleased?"

"Yeah. You bet. Darned pleased. I can't believe it."

"Believe it."

"Well . . ." He didn't know what to say next. Or do. This was cause for celebration, for turning handsprings, for letting out a war-whoop. Here was a girl who could have any man in Texas, any man in Colorado Territory, any man in the world, and she wanted him. And all he could do was sputter,

"Uh, uh . . ."

"It will soon be time for you to go."

"Oh. Yeah, that." For a while there he'd forgotten. She stood. "Would you like to kiss me for luck?"

Would he? He said, "Sure, you bet." He stood too. His hands were trembling when he put them on her shoulders.

Smiling that half-smile, she stepped closer.

A racket at the door jerked them apart.

Todd Kildow and Marietta Manahan looked at each other with questions on their faces.

She whispered, "How did they know?"

He could only shake his head.

His first thought was to climb out the window, but that wouldn't do. They knew he was in there, and they'd have a man, or men, waiting outside the window.

It was over. They wouldn't let him get away a second time. All over. He looked at Marietta Manahan with sad eyes and continued shaking his head. It was hopeless.

The racket came again, a kicking on the door.

She moaned, "Oh, Todd."

His shoulders slumped.

Suddenly, she moved. Grabbed the rifle that was standing in a corner, jacked the lever down. "I'm not going to let them take you. You're my man and by God they're not going to take you."

"Marrie. Marrie, for God's sake, don't shoot. They'll hang you." He grabbed the rifle, twisted it out of her hands. "Go back home, Marrie. Forget about me. I'm nothing but trouble."

The kicking continued.

Frustration brought tears to her eyes. "Goshdamn it. Damn it all."

"All right, now," Todd said, trying to be calm. "I'm going to open the door and stand back, and nobody is going to get hurt. All right?"

She stood there, tears running down her face, and nodded.

Todd Kildow slid the latch, opened the door and stepped back.

CHAPTER TWENTY-SEVEN

First to come through the door was J.D. Hays. He came through in a rush, staggered, stumbled and almost fell. His face was white with fear and his eyes were wild.

Todd jumped back out of the way. "What the hell?"

A small scream erupted from Marietta Manahan.

Hays was followed through the door by the Cheyenne Indian. His face was set in granite and he held the skinning knife in his right hand.

"Stop him!" Hays cried. "For the love of God, stop him. He's a bloodthirsty savage."

The Indian advanced toward Hays, holding the knife in front of himself in a knife-fighter's position.

"For God's sake, stop him."

It took a couple of seconds for Todd to realize what was happening, and then he stepped between the Indian and Hays. "Hold on, Pistol. Don't kill him. I need him alive."

The Indian stepped around Todd and put the point of the knife against Hay's chest, but didn't advance farther. Hays backed up, his face twisted in fear.

"He's a crazy savage. He wants to kill me."

"All right, all right." Todd got between the two

again. "Listen, Pistol, I don't blame you for wanting to kill him, but don't do it. Listen, I'll . . ." Suddenly he knew why the Indian had brought Hays to the cabin. "Oh, now I get it." A slow smile spread across his face.

"What is it, Todd? What's going on?"

To Hays, Todd said, "Sit down in that chair, Mister Hays, we wanta talk with you."

"Oh," Miss Manahan said, "now I get it too. Pistol put two and two together. He knows you are looking for a man, and he believes it's Mister Hays. He realizes you don't recognize the man and he wants to prove it to you."

Hays sat. His fingers were folded in his lap, twitching nervously. He was bareheaded and a bunch of dark hair stood straight up as if someone had grabbed a handful and lifted. His trimmed moustache was turned sideways over fear-twisted lips. "What are you going to do? Please don't let that savage cut me."

Standing over him, the Indian never took his eyes from Hays's face.

"We've got a few questions for you, Mister Hays. Do you feel like answering, or shall I let my Cheyenne friend lift your scalp?"

"No." Hays was near hysteria. "Don't let him touch me. I'll give you money."

Todd stood behind Hays, behind the chair. "Did you come through western Kansas a little over a year ago? With two other men?"

"Yeah. Yes."

"Did you shoot some Indians?"

"Yes, but they were savages. They would have shot us."

"Do you recognize this Indian?"

"No. Why should I?"

244

"He's one of the three you shot."

Hays started to jump up, but the point of the knife was raised to his chin. Immediately, he sat again. "He . . . he can't be. They are dead."

"He lived, and he is."

Scared eyes rolled around, trying to see Todd. "You're not going to let him cut me? Surely, you won't let him do anything? They were just savages."

"Savages." Marietta Manahan blurted the word. "Indians are human too. They don't want to die. They love and," she paused, "they hate."

"He hates your guts, Mister Hays. One signal from me and he'll cut your throat before he takes your scalp."

"Please, don't let him. I'll give you anything."

"Who else did you kill in western Kansas?"

"What? Nobody."

"Yes, you did. You killed my . . ." Todd shut his mouth a moment, then turned to the girl. "Marrie, will you fetch the marshal?"

"Yes." She grabbed a shawl from a nail on the wall and wrapped it around her shoulders. "I'll be right back." She closed the door behind her.

After she left, Todd lifted the stolen six-gun from the holster on his right hip, checked the loads, and kept it in his hand. He stood near the door, listening. "Just make yourself comfortable, Mister Hays. When the marshal gets here you're gonna tell him all about it."

"All about what? All we did was shoot some savages."

Todd stood next to the door, against the wall, the six-gun ready. The Indian kept his position. They waited.

Finally, he heard voices. A voice. A woman's voice. Marrie's. She was talking loudly, wanting him to

245

hear her coming. Todd flattened against the door.

"In here, marshal." The door opened and Marietta Manahan came through, followed by Deputy U.S. Marshal Garrick Ruhl.

The marshal had a gun in his hand. He stopped suddenly when he saw the Indian and then J.D. Hays.

Hays yelled, "Marshal, thank God. Look out."

"What in thunderation . . . ?" Garrick Ruhl started to spin around, then stiffened when he felt the bore of a gun in his back.

"Stand easy, Marshal." Todd reached around him and twisted the gun out of his hand. It occurred to him that this was the second time in two days he'd done that. "Just take a chair over there and listen. That's all we want you to do."

"I apologize, Mr. Ruhl," the girl said. "I had to get you here some way."

Garrick Ruhl's bushy eyebrows pulled together in a dark scowl. "You're threatening an officer of the law. The U.S. government don't take kindly to threats against an officer of the law."

"We mean you no harm," she said. "We need a witness, an impartial one. A witness with integrity."

"What's that Indian doing here? And what in Sam Hill do you all think you're doing?"

Keeping his gun pointed in the marshal's direction, Todd pulled out another chair. "Sit down. As soon as you listen to what this man has to say I'll give you your gun back and this one too. That's a promise."

"This is against the law, you know. You're already in a lot of trouble." He sat.

"Will you listen?"

"Make it quick."

"All right. Here's what's happened. Mister Hays here and two sidekicks rode through western Kansas a little over a year ago. They came up on three Indians and shot them down. One of the Indians survived. This one. He's been looking for the killers ever since he got well enough to travel.

"They were savages, Mr. Ruhl." J.D. Hays was keeping his voice under control now. He had the law on his side. "It's no crime to shoot Cheyennes."

Nodding toward the Indian, Todd said, "Ask him if it's no crime." When he got no answer, he went on, "Now, besides shooting three Indians, who else did you kill in western Kansas?"

"What? Nobody."

"How about a farm couple?"

"Wait a minute, now," the marshal put in. "Are you trying to prove that Mister Hays is one of the three men who murdered your folks?"

"That's exactly what I'm doing. He's going to admit it, ain't you, Mister Hays."

"I'll admit nothing."

Todd nodded at the Indian. "All right, Pistol. Show him what'll happen if he doesn't talk."

A quick flick of the wrist, and a small red streak appeared on Hays's left cheek. Hays screamed, a weird, high-pitched scream, like a woman's.

"Don't. For God's sake, stop him."

"You're a killer, Mister Hays. The kind of man who would murder a farm couple who never hurt anybody in their lives. My Cheyenne friend here is going to cut your throat from ear to ear."

"No. Please."

The Indian raised the knife so the point was against Hays' throat.

"Stop him. Please."

"Who else did you kill?"

"All right. We were hungry. We only wanted some food."

"You're a liar. My folks would never turn a hungry

247

man away. White or Indian. Why did you kill them?"

"We only wanted . . ."

Todd held up a hand. "Wait." He turned to the marshal. "I'm going to ask him some questions that only the guilty could answer. He'll be talking under fear for his life, but you'll know by the answers that he's telling the truth."

The marshal's mouth was clamped shut.

"All right now, Mister J.D. Hays, businessman, saloon owner, tell the marshal what happened." When there was hesitation, Todd added, "My friend here wants to stick that knife up your nose and see how far he can split it." Todd's voice was cold. "What happened? Why did you kill my folks?"

Hays's eyes crossed as they fixed on the knife. He rolled them toward the marshal, back to the knife. "We, uh, my partners saw a horse they wanted."

"What kind of a horse?"

"A black mare. We tried to buy the mare, but that sodbuster wouldn't sell her."

"I'll bet you tried to buy her. What happened?"

"My partners shot the farmer. One of them did."

"Then what?"

"We went to the house. A woman there was screaming and yelling and trying to run out the door."

Todd's throat tightened suddenly, and he couldn't go on. The vision of his mother . . . and his dad lying dead near the barn. He tried to talk, but only a strangling noise came out. Miss Manahan took over. She was calm, Cold, but calm.

"Did you shoot her, Mister Hays?"

The saloon owner wiped his cut cheek with the palm of his left hand. A tear ran down his face when he saw blood on his hand.

Marrie bored in, "Did you shoot her?"

"Yes. No. I mean Suggs did. One of my partners. I tried to talk him out of it, but he said maybe there was some money around."

"Was there?"

"Yes. In a jar in a cupboard."

"What else did you take?"

"Nothing. Well, yes. There was some fresh bread. We took some."

"Then what?"

"We got the mare and got away from there."

"Which way did you go?"

"West. We were going to Denver."

"What happened after that?"

"We camped by a river under some trees. Some-body snuck up on us and started shooting."

"What did you do?"

"I ran and got on my horse and got away."

"What happened to your partners?"

"I think they were shot."

A long pause, and Marietta Manahan turned to Todd. "Anything else, Todd?"

He had to clear his throat before he could talk. "No, I don't think so. How about you, Marshal?"

Garrick Ruhl's eyes were fixed on J.D. Hays's face. Fixed solid. He answered without moving his eyes. "No. I've got the rights of it."

"Here, Marshal." Todd handed over two guns.

Garrick Ruhl didn't move for a while. He con-tinued staring at J.D. Hays. The saloon owner sat perfectly still with the point of the knife at his throat. A tear ran down his cheek, across his trimmed moustache, and dripped off his chin.

Finally, the marshal stood. "Tell the Indian to put the knife away."

Todd held his right hand out, all fingers pointing down. He pushed the hand forward and brought it up. Shaking his head, the Cheyenne held his position.

"He wants to kill him," Todd said.

"I can stop him." The marshal raised his Colt six-gun.

"You do and you'll have to shoot me too," Todd said.

"And me." Miss Manahan moved quickly between the marshal and the Indian.

The lawman stood still.

"I'll try to make him understand," Todd said. He held his hand shoulder-high with the index and middle fingers together, and slowly raised the hand. Next he pointed at himself and then at the Indian. "We're friends," he said. "I need this man alive."

Face stony, jaws clamped shut, the Cheyenne's eyes went to Miss Manahan standing between him and the marshal's gun. He glanced at Todd, then back to the woman.

"Please," she said softly.

Slowly, he withdrew the knife, put it in its sheath and walked in his decorated moccasins to the door. His face never changed expressions. At the door he paused.

Whispering loudly, Marietta Manahan said, "Thank you, friend."

And he was gone.

J.D. Hays slumped in his chair and reached with a trembling hand for the cut on his cheek. His voice was weak. "Thank God." He fingered the cut and turned to the marshal. "Did you see what they did to me? They almost killed me. Did you see it?"

Two words came from Garrick Ruhl, "Shut up."

It was Marietta Manahan who spoke next. "Now

you know why Todd did what he did in Kansas. He tried to tell the sheriff there, but the sheriff wouldn't listen. What do you think?"

The marshal stroked his moustache with a forefinger. Then he said, "It sounds to me like what they call justifiable homicide. I'm no barrister and I ain't going to try to tell you what the law is in Kansas, but in the territories you wouldn't have been arrested."

Miss Manahan was emphatic. "The sheriff there is a pig-headed fool."

"Wa-al, I ain't gonna make no comment on that." Garrick Ruhl turned to Todd. "But you'll have to go back."

"Will you go with him and testify to what you heard tonight?"

"Sure, ma'am. It's my duty."

Todd asked, "What are you going to do with old Hays?"

"He'll have to go too. I'm placing him under arrest for murder."

"That will make four of us," Miss Manahan said. "I'm going."

A sigh came from the marshal. "It'll be a long trip. In those coaches. I'm dreading it." He sighed again. "But it's my duty."

"And it's going to be crowded," she said. "The four of us and any other passengers. In fact, some other passengers will have to wait for the next stage because of us."

"I know, ma'am."

"And how can you keep track of so many people? I mean two prisoners and me. Boy, you've got your work cut out for you, Marshal."

Shaking his head, Garrick Ruhl said, "Nobody told me this job was easy."

"It's darn nigh impossible. Like you said, it's a

long trip."

The marshal thought it over, stroking his moustache, and reached a decision. "Here's what. You, Todd Kildow, surrendered to me. I can't handle more than one prisoner at a time without help. And even if I did have help, we couldn't all get in those coaches. Now. You've got horses. Both of you. Will you give me your word you'll go to Prairie, Kansas and turn yourself in to the sheriff?"

"I will," Todd said.

"You'll be sorry if you don't," the lawman said. "You won't be so hard to find in the future. And I've got a hunch you and this young lady don't want to be fugitives from justice."

"You've got my word."

"All right. The stage line has got relay stations all along the way, so we'll get there ahead of you, but don't you waste any time. Understand?"

"Agreed."

"All right. I've got to lock this gentleman up. I hope I can find a better guard this time. Say, how did you get your hands untied, anyway?"

"I just kept working at it."

"We've got to build a jail in this town. That's gonna be my first project when I get back." He took J.D. Hays by the shirt collar and pulled him to his feet. "Come on, you."

Hays opened his mouth to speak, but was cut off immediately.

"Shut up. Don't say a word. Not one dang word."

"Shoo." Todd Kildow dropped into a kitchen chair.

"A double shoo." She stood before him, looking like a tramp in her baggy overalls and fluffed-up hair. And then she let out a signal of delight and raised both hands in the air like the winner in a box-fighting match. "Todd. It worked."

"Yeah." He grinned. "Everything I wanted to do, we've done." He looked up at her and his grin widened. "We've done it, Marrie."

"Of course. We're partners, aren't we?"

"Partners? Is that all?"

A half-smile and a mischievous glint appeared in her green eyes. "No. There's more."

He pulled her down onto his lap.

They talked far into the night, making plans. Happy plans. They would go on horseback to Prairie, Kansas. His pack horse could easily carry two bedrolls and enough chuck for two. They would stop in a town called Colorado City on the east side of the mountains, and they would be married. Later they would go into the cattle business in western Kansas and maybe expand into Colorado Territory.

"Todd." She took his face between her hands and kissed him soundly. "For the first time in many years, I'm pleased with life, with the whole world."

That was when a terrible, blood-chilling scream split the night and awakened half the town of White River.

A dozen men had gathered at the cabin-jail by the time Todd and Marietta Manahan got there. Some were still buttoning their shirts and suspenders. Marshal Garrick Ruhl ran up, breathing hard from the run.

"Here, now. What's going on?"

A man in jackboots and wool pants sat on the

253

ground in front of the cabin rubbing the side of his head. A pitiable groaning and sobbing came from inside the cabin. A lighted lamp was on the floor. The marshal squatted in front of the man.

"What happened, Joseph?"

Joseph rubbed the side of his head. "I didn't see 'im and I didn't hear 'im. Somebody clubbed me upside the head and then I heard somebody screamin' bloody murder in there."

A half-dozen men tried to squeeze through the cabin door at once. Someone swore, "Jaysus Jones." Garrick Ruhl pushed his way in, grabbed the lantern and held it close to J.D. Hays. Hays was sitting on the floor. Blood covered his head and shoulders. He was groaning and crying.

"Good gawd amighty," Ruhl said in a half-whisper. "Go get the doctor. Run."

"Jumpin' Jesus. Scalped 'im."

"Holy mother of . . . Who coulda done it?"

"Scalped 'im alive."

"Yup. Shore did. Sliced 'er off, right off the top."

"Injun fashion. Musta been that Injun that's been prowlin' around here."

"Did somebody run for the doc?"

"Yeah. He's comin'."

Two men hurried up. One was young with uncombed hair and wearing a long nightshirt. He had pants and lace-up shoes on under the nightshirt, and he carried a small satchel. Men stepped aside to make room for him.

The doctor bent over J.D. Hays, held the lantern closer, said, "Hmm," and straightened up. "We'll have to get him to bed."

"What is it, Doc?"

"Looks like a piece of scalp was removed."

"What'd I say? That injun scalped 'im."

254

"Is that right, Doc? Is that what happened?"

"It appears to be what happened. Neat work. Just took some scalp and hair from the back portion of the head. A surgeon couldn't have done better."

"Is he gonna live?"

"Probably. We'll have to get him to bed and clean the wound and apply some antiseptic. He'll have a very sore head for a time, but he should recover."

They followed the wagon road east out of town. The air was clean and fresh, the sky a bright blue. Summer flowers spotted the meadows and hillsides with red, yellow and purple. Todd Kildow was riding his good bay horse and leading the pack horse. Marietta Manahan was on her dun. His Remington was on his right hip, and her Winchester was carried in a boot under her right leg.

"We can take our time now, Todd."

"Plenty of time. The doctor said old Hays won't be able to travel for at least a week."

"How far did you say it is to Colorado City, or whatever that town is called?"

"Two days."

The road stretched up a long hill and wound through tall spruce and pine. A roadchuck, sitting on a pile of small boulders, jerked its tail and chirped.

"I want to get spruced up, Todd. In a dress and everything. Do you mind waiting until then?"

Grinning, he said, "I've waited a long time for a woman like you, Marrie. Another couple of days won't hurt."

The horses were happy to be out of the pens and moving, and they stepped right along. Tall timber gave way to an open meadow with a willow-lined creek. They stopped and let the horses drink.

"We all got what we wanted back there, didn't we, Todd, even Pistol?"

"Yep. He can go back to his people now, or wherever he wants to go, and know he got his revenge. He's got a scalp to prove it."

Mounted again, they followed the road out of the flatland, and up another long hill. At the top they stopped to let the horses blow.

"Look." She was pointing to the south.

A man sat motionless on a horse a quarter-mile away, on the edge of a stand of aspen. The man had long hair and was bareheaded. He waved.

"It's him, Todd. He's waving at us."

Todd took off his hat and waved it over his head. Miss Manahan did the same.

"Will we ever see him again, Todd?"

"I don't know. I doubt it."

"I'll never forget him."

"Neither will I."

The horseman waved one more time, then turned his horse and disappeared into the woods. Todd Kildow watched until he was out of sight.

"So long, my friend."